Still Glides the Stream

Still Glides the Stream

D. E. Stevenson

HOLT, RINEHART AND WINSTON

NEW YORK

In this Romance of the Borders the characters and places are entirely imaginary and no reference to any living person is intended; but it is impossible to avoid using names connected with the district by history and tradition. The author can only repeat that if the name of any living person has been "borrowed" it is by inadvertence and not of design.

First Edition published in the United States in 1959.
Second edition published in Great Britain in 1977; and in the United States in 1979 by Holt, Rinehart and Winston, 383 Madison Avenue, New York, New York 10017.

Library of Congress Cataloging in Publication Data
Stevenson, Dorothy Emily, 1892-1973.
Still glides the stream.
I. Title.
PZ3.S8472Sr 1979 [PR6037.T458] 823'.9'12
ISBN 0-03-052086-x 79-1918

Printed in the United States of America
10 9 8 7 6 5 4 3 2 1

Contents

I thought of Thee, my partner and my guide,
As being past away.—Vain sympathies!
For backward, Duddon, as I cast my eyes,
I see what was, and is, and will abide;
Still Glides the Stream, and shall forever glide;
The Form remains, the Function never dies.

Valedictory Sonnet to the River Duddon
WILLIAM WORDSWORTH

PART ONE

Broadmeadows

Chapter 1

I travell'd among unknown men
In lands beyond the sea . . .

WILL HASTIE remembered this scrap of poetry as he rode
up the hill. The words came into his head—it was
almost as if somebody had said them—but he could not
remember their context nor who had written them. No
doubt he would remember later when he was not trying;
that was the way one's brain worked.

For years Will had travelled among unknown men;
now that he was home he could not make up his mind
whether he felt like Rip van Winkle or whether he felt
as if he had been here yesterday riding his pony through
these self-same woods. The trees had not changed a
whit—they were hard-wood trees, beeches and oaks and
chestnuts—the turf of the ride was as smooth and green
as ever, and when Will emerged from the woods on to
the open moor he could see Cloudhill with a small white
puffy cloud like a scrap of cotton-wool hovering over its
summit. There was nearly always a cloud—sometimes
small and white, sometimes dark and thundery—hovering over Cloudhill. Looking at it now, Will remembered the day he had climbed the hill with his father;
it was a clear sunny day but when they reached the top

the cloud came down and enveloped them in its damp embrace. It had been quite an uncanny experience and if he had not been with his father it would have alarmed him considerably.

There were queer stories about Cloudhill. Some of the local people would tell you that the cloud was a device of " Auld Hornie " and he could call it up out of a clear summer sky. The hill-top belonged to him—so they said—and there were folk in Torfoot who would swear to having seen Auld Hornie himself, complete with horns, standing upon a rock near the summit—and laughing. Other folk, less credulous, declared that Auld Hornie of Cloudhill was no more than a mountain goat.

Will did not know which of these theories to believe but his father was there so it did not matter. " Dear me, it's like a wet blanket," said Mr. Hastie cheerfully. " We'll have to hold hands, Will." So they had come down holding hands and in a surprisingly few minutes had emerged into sunshine.

It was odd to remember that little incident after all these years (and to remember it so clearly) but all sorts of odd and unrelated memories were crowding into Will's mind to-day. On his right was a cluster of rocks rising from amongst the trees in a conical formation. It had been Will's look-out tower, for although it was not really very high it was so situated that it gave one a view into the next valley where the river ran and where Langford House lay upon the other side of the ford. Langford had been Will's second home, and the young Elliot Murrays—Rae and Patience—had been more like a brother and a sister than ordinary friends, so although Will was an only child and his father had often been away on business Will had never felt lonely.

Never? Well, hardly ever! thought Will . . . for now he remembered an occasion when he had felt very lonely indeed. It was during the Christmas holidays, and Will had been in contact with a miserable child who was discovered to be suffering from mumps, so he was debarred from visiting Langford—he was exiled for three weeks! Will formed the habit of climbing the huddle of rocks and looking down at the house by the river. After the first day of his discovery Will took a small spy-glass with him and this brought Langford nearer. He could see old Brown in the kitchen-garden, and noted (with a child's detachment) that old Brown did not work nearly as hard as the gardener at Broadmeadows—MacLaggan by name. He could see Colonel Elliot Murray go out in his car and Rae and Patty come home from their morning walk. Will liked to visit his look-out tower about four o'clock in the afternoon and to watch the lights go on . . . and especially to watch for the light to go on in the window of the play-room in the attic where Rae and Patty had their tea and indulged in all sorts of interesting pastimes.

The light went on and immediately afterwards somebody—either Rae or Patty—pulled down the scarlet blind; the window became a bright-red rectangle shining in the gathering darkness. All the other windows in Langford House had yellow blinds, so even when it was quite dark, even when it was a little misty, there was no mistaking which was the window of the play-room. Later, when his quarantine was over and Will had been welcomed back to Langford with open arms, he told Rae and Patty about his discovery and Rae suggested a use for the scarlet blind.

" It can be a signal," said Rae. " You can watch for it, can't you? I mean if Patty and I have got to go to that frightful tea-fight to-morrow we'll pull the blind half-way down and you'll know it's no use coming—see? "

Will saw. " Half-mast," he agreed nodding.

After that there was a regular code of signals—the blind could even be used for morse—and, although it would have been easier to telephone messages between Broadmeadows and Langford, it was far more romantic to send them by way of the blind—as any properly minded child will know.

What fun we had! thought Will, with a nostalgic sigh for his childhood. How lucky I was to have Langford—and Rae and Patty to play with!

2

So far everything had looked the same to Will; the trees, the rocks, Cloudhill with its cap of white; but when he looked westwards towards Craigrowan Will saw that the plantation of conifers which he remembered as tiny seedlings had grown into fine young trees. (That shows you! thought Will, gazing across the valley in astonishment.) Of course he knew perfectly well that he had not been home for twelve years, but all the same he was astonished at the transformation.

It was almost exactly twelve years since Will had been at Broadmeadows. His last visit had been during the war when he had been wounded—not very seriously—

and had been granted a fortnight's sick-leave. The first few days of leave had been a period of absolute bliss, but after that he was not quite so happy.

One evening when Will and his father were sitting in the smoking-room together Mr. Hastie had said quite suddenly, " I shall have to tell you, Will. You won't like it, but it can't be helped; I've decided to let Broadmeadows."

" Let Broadmeadows! " echoed Will in horrified tones.

" I'm afraid so, my boy. It's a bit of a wrench but we must face facts. I told you I've been offered that post in London—and you've got your profession. You've made up your mind to stay on in the Army after the war is over, haven't you? So you see it would mean this place standing empty for months on end. There doesn't seem much sense in that—and what's more we can't afford it. If we let Broadmeadows the money will put us on our legs again."

Will said reluctantly, " Well, perhaps if you can get a good offer——"

" But I have! That's the point. I've got an extremely good offer. It's a fellow called Levison, a business-man from Manchester. He wants a place on the Borders with a bit of shooting and fishing. As a matter of fact I wasn't too keen—couldn't bear the idea somehow—but Levison is determined to have Broadmeadows and doesn't seem to mind what he pays for it . . . so there you are! Quite honestly I see no reasonable alternative. You see, Will, I want to come home to Broadmeadows when I retire and I shall want money to put the whole place into repair. The estate really needs a good deal of money spent on repairs."

This was true, every word of it. So the old family estate had been let for ten years to Mr. Levison, and Will had spent his infrequent periods of leave at his father's flat in London. In a way it had been very pleasant; Will and his father were cronies, they had done the town together and enjoyed it, but both of them had always looked forward to going home.

Two years ago Mr. Hastie had retired and returned to Broadmeadows and now Will also had retired for although he was only thirty-five he had had his fill of travelling in lands beyond the sea and was glad to take advantage of the special terms offered to officers on the reorganisation of the Army. Will wanted to return to his own place and become a farmer.

It was difficult to believe that he was here " for keeps " —almost too good to be true! Here he was and here he would remain for the rest of his life; he was his own master, no longer at the beck and call of those mythical beings at the War Office who seemed to delight in sending you off to the end of the world at the most inconvenient moments.

Spring time is the most beautiful time of the year in the Scottish Borders. It comes slowly and shyly as if it feared that Jack Frost might return and give it a mischievous nip. The tender buds unfold in the pale golden sunshine and in sheltered nooks you may find a scatter of yellow primroses or some purple violets hiding amongst their green leaves. To-day was that sort of day, beautiful and peaceful. The light breeze rustled in the grasses and far in the distance Will heard the call of a grouse. There was no other sound to disturb the perfect stillness.

After a bit Will rode on across the moor and presently

came to the dry-stone dyke which marked the boundary of his father's property. He noticed that the gate, which had always been a ramshackle affair, had been replaced by a sound one. That's the stuff! thought Will in approval. Father was right; it was worth while letting the place and getting the money to put things in order. We'll get everything ship-shape—and we'll make it pay. The farms ought to pay if they're properly modernised —and I don't see why we shouldn't plant conifers. I must learn, thought Will. I must find out about forestry . . .

3

Will's head was full of ideas as he rode down the steep path to the river but they vanished when he rounded an outcrop of rocks, for coming towards him along the path was Colonel Elliot Murray; there was no mistaking the tall thin figure of the laird. Twelve years had laid their mark upon him; his hair which had been iron-grey was now silver and his shoulders were not so straight and soldierly. Twelve years and the loss of his only son were enough to age any man, so Will ought to have been prepared to see a change in him . . . but Will was not prepared.

Why—he's an old man! thought Will—and his heart contracted strangely, for ever since he could remember Colonel Elliot Murray had been his hero, and heroes should never grow old. Will thought there was nobody like the Colonel—nobody so brave, nobody so full of integrity, nobody so good and kind. (Nor was Will singular in this respect for everybody in the district was fond of him and proud of him; he was pointed out to visitors as one of the "sights" of Torfoot. "That's the laird," people would say. " He won the V.C. in the First War—but there's no side about him. He's the same to everybody. Take a good look at him for you'll not see his like in the whole of Scotland.")

By this time they had approached near enough for the Colonel to recognise Will and to wave and hasten his steps.

" My dear fellow! " he exclaimed. " My dear Will, this is a delightful surprise! Your father told me you were coming but I had no idea it would be so soon . . ."

Will slipped off the pony's back and they shook hands.

" We were all so glad when your father came back," continued the Colonel. " Mr. Levison was a very pleasant neighbour but it seemed all wrong to have strangers at Broadmeadows—we couldn't get used to it at all. And now you're home! Are you glad to be home, Will? "

A few minutes ago Will had been glad—indeed almost unbearably happy—but now he was almost unbearably sad. He had known it would be distressing to meet Colonel Elliot Murray but he had not realised it would be so heart-rending. That's what it was—heart-rending. He was almost ashamed of being here, alive and well, standing upon the hillside and talking to Rae's father (or rather, *not* talking to Rae's father because there was such a large lump in his throat that he couldn't speak). Will was more upset now, at this moment, than he had been when he first heard that Rae had been killed in action. *That* had been bad enough in all conscience, but it was war-time and life was a precarious affair;

people were being killed every day; his own life was in constant danger. In war you can't go on grieving even for your best friend. Now it was different and the grief and misery rose like a tidal wave and nearly swamped him. Here he was, home again, and Rae was not here! If he went down to Langford House, which he could see lying peaceful and secure in the hollow by the river, Rae would not be there. The play-room in the attic would be empty. Rae's fishing-rods would be stacked tidily in the corner; the table would be clear of books and papers and bottles of gun-oil and boxes of cartridges and all the other impedimenta with which it had been cluttered in bygone days . . .

" Are you coming to lunch, Will? " asked Colonel Elliot Murray.

" Not to-day, sir," replied Will, finding his voice with difficulty. " You see it's my first day at home———"

" Of course! How foolish of me! Your father will want you to have lunch with him . . . but come as soon as you can and tell us all your news. Patty will be delighted to see you, and—and Margaret."

" How is Mrs. Elliot Murray? "

" Wonderfully well. She forgets things, you know; so you—you mustn't be surprised—but otherwise wonderfully well. She won't have forgotten you, of course. You were always a favourite of hers."

It was difficult to know what to say, except that he would come as soon as he could—possibly on Friday.

" That's right, Will. Come on Friday," said the Colonel. " Friday is Patty's day for practising the organ at St. Martin's, but she'll be home in plenty of time for lunch."

Chapter 2

FRIDAY WAS a cloudy day with scatters of rain and bursts of sunshine. It was weather which fitted perfectly with Will's feelings. The truth was he could not make up his mind if he wanted to go to Langford or not. Of course he wanted to see Patty . . . but lunch would be a miserable business.

" You're sure you can spare me, Father? " asked Will as he rose from the breakfast table. He had asked the question before and had been answered in the affirmative. This time Mr. Hastie put down *The Scotsman* and looked at Will gravely.

" Better get it over," said Mr. Hastie. " Take the pony and ride down to Langford. You'd much better get it over."

" Get it over? "

" Yes, it's got to be done, you know. Never any good putting things off. I felt the same when I came home to Broadmeadows—if that's any consolation to you."

" Do you mean—— "

Mr. Hastie nodded. " Langford is—is sort of— empty." He hesitated and then added, " But remember it's eleven years since Rae was killed so they've had time to get used to it."

" Are they—used to it? " asked Will lingering by his chair.

"People have got to get used to things—or else go off their heads. It took me a long time to get used to the empty feeling in this house when your mother died. You don't remember her of course?"

"Not really," admitted Will.

"It took me a long time," repeated Mr. Hastie. "As a matter of fact the emptiness was so unbearable that I decided to move—I thought it might be better somewhere else—but it seemed like running away—and Mary admired courage—so I stuck to my guns. I had you and I had my work so I struggled through. There was a bad patch when you went off to Glenalmond but I got through that too." Mr. Hastie took up his paper and added, "Always stick to your guns, Will."

"Yes," said Will. He would have liked to say more but he was so astonished that he was almost speechless. He and his father had always been the best of friends but he had never had an inkling of his father's feelings —had never suspected that his father had any feelings at all.

Why didn't I? thought Will as he went out to fetch the pony. It must have been frightful for him. Why didn't I understand? I could have been nicer to him, thought Will, remorsefully.

Of course there was no need for Will to feel remorse, for he had always been extremely "nice" to his father. He had been too young when his mother died to grieve for her so it had never occurred to him that his father might miss her companionship. Children take their circumstances for granted and it had seemed quite natural to Will that he had no mother. Perhaps he would have missed her, or at least felt a blank in his life, if it had not been for Lucy, who had come to Broadmeadows to look after Mrs. Hastie in her last illness and had stayed on to look after her baby son. Lucy had been quite a young girl in those days and not very experienced but what she lacked in knowledge she had made up for in love. Lucy had stayed with the Hasties, father and son, until Will was able to look after himself and then had left to be married—she had gone to Glasgow and disappeared from view.

Will had not thought of Lucy for years but now he remembered her and realised suddenly how much he owed her. I wonder where she is, he thought. I wonder what she's doing. Perhaps I could find out and write to her or something. It would be nice to see Lucy again. I'm home now, thought Will, as he heaved the saddle on to the pony's back and adjusted the girths, there's all the time in the world to look up old friends.

Having made this decision he felt easier in his mind and was free to think of his immediate problem: should he take the direct route to Langford—through the woods and over the hill and across the river by the ford—or should he go round by the bridge? There had been rain in the night so perhaps it would be wiser to stick to the road to-day. If this had been his own pony he would not have hesitated, for Clive had known the way to Langford as well as he knew his own stable, and the two of them had often taken the ford when most people would have shunned it, but dear old Clive had been dead for years and this somewhat sluggish beast was an unknown quantity. Will had no wish to arrive at Langford House soaked to the skin!

2

The little town of Torfoot lies clustered about the bridge; it is a pleasant little place, with a narrow, winding street, a few remarkably good shops and an old-fashioned hotel much patronised by anglers. Will knew it well, of course, but he had not been here since his return and was surprised to find it so small. Everything seemed to have shrunk and Torfoot which had dwelt in his recollection as a reasonably sized town was scarcely more than a village. He was surprised also, and rather touched, to discover that quite a number of people remembered him —or perhaps they recognised his father's pony! At any rate he was greeted by several residents whose names he had forgotten and whose faces he remembered only vaguely. He was greeted and welcomed and his future plans discussed and approved.

There are two churches in Torfoot; the Established Church which stands four-square in the centre of the town and St. Martin's Episcopal Church which is built upon a little knoll near the river. Most people refer to St. Martin's as " The English Church " for the services are the same, or almost the same, as the Church of England, but in doing so they are mistaken for both Churches are of Scottish origin.

Will knew this. From his earliest days he had been acquainted with the miserable history of the two Scottish Churches and what he did not know about the Covenanters and the Jacobites was scarcely worth knowing; he could have passed an examination upon the battles of Rullion Green, Philiphaugh and Bothwell Brig. Mr. Hastie, an ardent Jacobite and therefore an ardent Episcopalian, was wont to expatiate upon the atrocities committed by the Covenanters, but it had always seemed to Will that the Covenanters were not much worse than their opponents for whichever party happened to be in the ascendant persecuted the other with equal ferocity. Now, however, all that is forgotten; the Presbyterians and the Episcopalians live in peace and amity, attending one another's Whist Drives and spending generously at one another's Sales of Work . . . or at least that is the way of it in Torfoot . . .

As Will passed the little knoll upon which St. Martin's is built he heard the sound of the organ and remembered that Colonel Elliot Murray had said Patty always practised on Friday mornings. He decided it would be good to see Patty, and especially good to see Patty alone (he could find out a little about the situation at Langford before appearing at the luncheon table); so he dismounted and led the pony up the path and tied it to one of the iron rings at the side of the church which had been placed there long ago for this very purpose. Having done so Will stood for a few moments in the porch looking round at the well-known landmarks.

The view from here was beautiful. Below lay the little town with its grey stone buildings and blue slate roofs; the river ran through it, spanned by the bridge, and wandered away down the valley in sweeping curves as it made its way to the sea. Eastwards, and scarcely a mile distant, was the cluster of trees which hid Langford House—hid it completely except for the chimneys, one of which was smoking lazily in the still air. The whole scene, so peaceful and familiar, was ringed about with fat, comfortable hills which met the sky in rounded contours.

Like cushions, thought Will vaguely. That's what they are—really. That's what makes Torfoot such a safe cosy sort of place to live.

3

Presently Will pushed open the heavy door of the church and went in.

Patty was playing " Jesu, Joy of Man's Desiring." He had heard her playing the organ before, long ago when she was scarcely more than a child, but this was different for Patty was no longer a child. She had been through deep waters. He went quietly up the aisle and sat down in a pew near the organ. Tears came to his eyes as he listened, for this was a prayer from a woman in distress—and the woman was Patty. Was she still grieving for Rae?

When at last the music ceased Will did not move; he scarcely knew that Patty had stopped playing. The empty church seemed full of music, for it is that sort of music: the sort of music that goes on long after it has stopped.

Presently Patty turned to find another book and saw him. " Who—who is it? " she asked uncertainly.

" It's only me," said Will, rising and coming forward.

" Will! Oh Will, you frightened me! "

" I'm sorry. I didn't want you to stop—that's all."

" I always practise on Friday mornings."

Will nodded. " I know. Don't stop, Patty. I'll wait

if you don't mind and we can walk up to Langford together. I'm coming to lunch."

She held out her hand and he gave it a gentle squeeze.

"I've finished," she told him. "I was just enjoying myself. I could play *that* with my eyes shut. It's nice, isn't it?"

"Nice" seemed a poor word to describe it, but all the same Will agreed. "Very nice," he said.

"Oh Will!" she exclaimed. "I haven't said I'm terribly pleased to see you—but I am."

"So am I," said Will. "I mean it's lovely to see you again—and you're just the same."

She was the same Patty. She still looked exactly like herself, with her small straight nose, her broad white forehead and her curving generous mouth, and she still wore her brown curly hair cut short like a child. Her skin was unusually white for a brown-haired girl and her eyes were unusually blue. In the old days Patty had been plump; now she was slender which made her seem taller, but that was the only difference. Later Will was to revise his first impression a little but not much.

In the old days, when they were children it had never struck Will that Rae and Patty were like each other, but now he saw the family resemblance. Rae's eyes had been the same colour—gentian blue—and set widely apart, he had had the same straight nose and broad forehead, the same shape of head. His hair had been different of course, it had been honey-coloured and very thick and tufty and in spite of all his efforts to brush it down it had rarely looked as tidy as he had wished. Seeing Patty had brought back the memory of Rae very clearly to Will's mind.

26

"We're having your favourite pudding," said Patty as she gathered up the music and put it away in the cupboard. "At least it used to be your favourite—lemon meringue."

"It's still my favourite pudding."

"You haven't changed."

"Not in puddings——"

"Not in anything," said Patty looking up at him and smiling. Then her smile faded and she added in a low voice, "Everybody else has changed."

"Your mother has—has lost her memory."

"It's more than that, Will. She's lost—herself," said Patty with a little catch in her breath. "At least—I think so—but you'll see."

"You're worrying about her."

"I'm much more worried about Daddy. She's quite happy in her own queer way, but he's awfully miserable, poor darling—and he's got so old and frail and—and worn! Will, I want you to tell me honestly what you think about them."

He said he would and added, "If there's anything I can do to help . . ."

"Nobody can help much," she said sadly. "But you knew them so well, long ago. If I can just talk to you it will help."

They came out of church together and Will untied the pony.

"Not like Clive, is he?" said Patty changing the subject.

"No, he's awfully dull," replied Will. "I shall have to look about for a more interesting beast when I have time."

27

"Poor Duffer," said Patty with a little smile. "It's rather a shame to say he's dull. Who could be anything but dull with a name like that?"

Will had been about to say that he had had no idea what the pony was called; his father had referred to the animal as "the pony." ("Take the pony, Will," Mr. Hastie had said.) But before Will could explain this curious circumstance his eyes were caught by Patty's left hand which was stroking poor Duffer's nose and by the unexpected glitter of diamonds on her engagement finger.

"Are you—engaged—to somebody?" he asked.

"Yes, it's the only nice thing that has happened. Of course we can't be married for ages—I couldn't leave the parents and Hugo has his mother to think of—but we can wait."

"Hugo?"

"Yes, my cousin. I don't think you ever saw Hugo."

"I never even heard of him," declared Will.

By this time they were on the road to Langford, walking along together with Duffer following in his resigned and obedient manner. Certainly Duffer was no bother—you could say that of him.

"There was a family feud," explained Patty. "That's why Hugo never came to Langford in the old days. Of course if he had come to Langford you would have seen him. Hugo's father was Daddy's younger brother and they fell out about something—I don't know what it was. Then Uncle James got ill and Daddy went to see him and it was all made up. That's all I know."

"Oh, I see," said Will.

"Hugo doesn't know any more than I do, but it

doesn't matter. Those sort of things are better forgotten, aren't they?"

"Yes, I suppose so."

Patty hesitated and then continued, "When Rae was killed Hugo wrote a very nice letter to Daddy so we asked him to come and stay—and he came. After that he came several times and—and we liked each other. That was how it happened. You'll like Hugo. Everybody likes Hugo, he's a dear."

Will said nothing and for a few moments they walked on in silence.

"Langford is entailed of course," added Patty.

"Yes, of course," agreed Will. He said it in a matter-of-fact sort of voice, but his voice belied his feelings, which were extremely confused and uncomfortable. Langford was entailed—well, of course! Broadmeadows was entailed. All these old family places were entailed. Everybody knew that . . . so, some day, Langford would belong to this unknown cousin. Will had never thought of such a thing but now he realised that he was very silly not to have thought of it. Langford would belong to "Hugo," and Patty would marry the fellow, and they would live happily ever after. Patty had said, "You'll like Hugo," and had said it with conviction, but Will had a feeling that he would not like Hugo at all. He did not quite know why.

"They live in Wiltshire," continued Patty. "Bellstead is almost as big as Langford—and beautifully kept. Hugo lives there with his mother and looks after the estate. He knows all the modern methods of farming because after the war he went to Cambridge and took a degree in Agriculture. They have a dairy herd and they grow fruit and vegetables for the London market. It's quite a big thing and pays awfully well. Hugo says he could make Langford pay; it needs modernising, that's all."

Will had thought exactly the same about Broadmeadows, and already had made plans about learning how to run the farms on modern lines, so it was somewhat unreasonable of him to feel so annoyed with Hugo for his plans to modernise Langford—but Will was in an unreasonable state of mind.

" Modernise Langford! " he exclaimed in disgust.

" Yes, it's a thing called Work Study. You arrange everything to save labour and you install modern equipment. Hugo can tell you all about it when he comes."

Patty hesitated, but Will said nothing.

" Perhaps your father wouldn't like it? " suggested Patty doubtfully. " Uncle James didn't like it much. I mean Hugo had to be very tactful about it. He couldn't really get on with his plans until Uncle James died. He died quite suddenly."

(Arsenic, thought Will—but he still remained silent.)

" Hugo has no brothers and sisters," continued Patty. " He lives at Bellstead with his mother—but I told you that, didn't I? After we were engaged I went and stayed at Bellstead and she was very nice to me."

" Well, of course! Why shouldn't she be nice to to you? " demanded Will.

" Oh, I don't know. I just had a feeling that it was nice of her to be nice—if you see what I mean. She thinks Hugo is marvellous—and of course he is," added Patty hastily.

" Does your father like him? "

"Yes, of course. Everybody likes him."

Will felt inclined to say it was all very suitable but managed to refrain. It was all too suitable, he thought. Things just didn't happen like that. Here was the long-lost heir turning up at exactly the right moment and instead of being an absolute rotter he was *persona grata* with everybody; he was competent and experienced in the management of a big estate and Patty would marry him. Everybody was pleased—and no wonder. It was an admirable arrangement.

"He's coming quite soon," said Patty cheerfully. "Of course he's frightfully busy and doesn't get away very often, but he comes whenever he can."

The subject of Hugo lasted until they arrived at Langford House by which time Will was heartily sick of Hugo—it was a silly name anyway, he thought.

Chapter 3

HAVING STABLED Duffer Will went to wash in the downstairs bathroom. Already he could sense the queer empty feeling in the house. He had washed here so often—hundreds of times—thousands of times—with Rae. They had washed their dirty hands in the same basin, squabbled amicably over the soap and dried their hands on the roller-towel which hung on the back of the door.

It was all so clearly in Will's mind that he could scarcely believe Rae was not there, just behind him, and he almost expected to receive a friendly buffet and to hear Rae's voice telling him to hurry up or they would be late for lunch.

Will found his hostess sitting in the morning-room. He was surprised to see that she looked exactly the same as he remembered—scarcely a day older.

" Dear Will, how nice! " said Mrs. Elliot Murray. " You haven't been to see us for quite a long time."

" I've just come home, you know," he told her.

" Yes. You've been abroad, haven't you? "

" Yes," agreed Will. He was relieved at this greeting for he had not known what to expect. It was obvious, of course, that Mrs. Elliot Murray did not realise that she had not seen him for twelve years (she had greeted him as if she had not seen him for twelve weeks) but apart from that he could see nothing wrong—and that was a mere detail.

"I hope you've got a nice long leave," she continued, smiling at him kindly.

"I've retired," said Will. "I've left the Army. I'm a farmer now—or at least I'm going to learn to be a farmer."

Mrs. Elliot Murray nodded. "Much better," she said. "So nice for your father to have you. Sometimes I think he's a little lonely. Come and sit down and tell me all your news."

She was so absolutely normal that Will's strung-up feelings relaxed and he sat down beside her quite comfortably. He had always been very fond of "Aunt Margaret" (as he had called her) so it was easy to talk to her in the old way.

"Patty will be here soon," said Mrs. Elliot Murray. "She'll be so delighted to see you. Unfortunately Rae is away just now. I can't remember where he is . . ." Her face looked sad for a moment, sad and bewildered— then suddenly it brightened and she exclaimed, "But Patty will know! Patty must write and tell him you're here and then perhaps he'll come home. It would be lovely if Rae came home, wouldn't it?"

"Yes," said Will.

"You'd like to see him, wouldn't you?"

"Yes," said Will again.

"Patty will write," said Mrs. Elliot Murray happily. "Or perhaps Thomas should write to the colonel and explain why we want Rae home so badly. I'm sure if Thomas wrote a nice letter to the colonel he would give him leave."

Will rose. He could not sit there a moment longer. He said, " I see there's sherry here. Would you like me to give you a glass, Aunt Margaret? "

" No dear, but you have some. It was silly of me not to offer you sherry—but you don't need to be offered things here, do you? "

Will was pouring out the sherry when Patty came in.

" Lunch! " said Patty. " Daddy's just coming. He said not to wait."

2

Will had dreaded the ordeal of lunch, but it was not as bad as he had expected for there was plenty to talk about. They wanted to hear what he had been doing— all about everything as Patty put it. Mrs. Elliot Murray said very little but seemed to be listening with interest to the conversation. Occasionally her mind wandered and she asked a question which already had been answered; once she drifted into the past and asked Will when he was going back to Glenalmond.

" Oh, I've left Glenalmond, you know," said Will quite naturally.

" Oh, of course, how silly of me! "

" Have you met the Hestons yet? " asked Patty hastily. " They're awfully nice. You must meet them, Will."

" Ask them over some day when Will is coming," suggested the Colonel.

Will was not particularly interested in the Hestons but he was anxious to keep the conversation running in case Mrs. Elliot Murray began to talk about Rae. (She had said that Patty—or Thomas—must write and arrange for Rae to come home and although she seemed to have forgotten all about it there was no knowing when she might remember.) This being so Will made searching inquiries about the new neighbours and learned that the family consisted of Mr. and Mrs. Heston, two grown-up daughters and a young son.

" I hope they'll settle down," said Patty. " They're English and I think they're finding things a bit strange. They had to leave their home because it was near an airfield and the jets were so noisy."

" It's quiet enough here," commented Will.

" Perhaps a wee bit too quiet," nodded Patty. " Brenda likes it all right. She's taking over the Torfoot Guide Company and making a good job of it."

" She's very plain, poor girl," said Mrs. Elliot Murray, who had the disconcerting habit of emerging suddenly from her fog and chipping into the conversation when one least expected it.

" Plain! " cried Patty. " Oh no, Mummy! Brenda isn't plain. She's a perfect dear."

The Colonel chuckled. He said, " If Patty is fond of people they're never plain. They might even be downright ugly but Patty would still think them handsome. . . . And of course if they were keen on Guides she would think them as beautiful as the day."

" I'm inclined to agree with Patty," said Will thoughtfully.

" So does Daddy, really," Patty declared. " I don't mean Guides of course, but anything he's interested in . . . besides, Brenda has simply beautiful eyes."

" And mousy hair," murmured the Colonel.

"You're teasing!" said Patty smiling. "And anyhow I like mice—so there!"

It was not a very logical conversation but Will was enjoying himself now. He said, "Well, that's Brenda. What about the other members of the family?"

"Daddy likes Mr. Heston," said Patty.

The Colonel nodded. "I find him interesting. We haven't got much in common, of course, because our lives have been so different; he was a stockbroker and although he has retired he still keeps his eye on the market and buys and sells stock on his own account. I gather he makes a good deal. He offered to give me some advice about my own small investments—which was decent of him. I know nothing about these things," added the Colonel vaguely.

"You ought to be careful, sir," suggested Will.

The Colonel nodded. "Oh, of course. But Heston knows what he's talking about—you can see that. Another thing he told me—rather interesting really. His partner's name is Murray and, when Heston said he was building a house near Torfoot, Murray said he had cousins there—distant cousins whom he had never seen."

"Not us?" asked Patty eagerly but with a deplorable lack of grammar.

"It might well be," replied the Colonel. "I thought I would find out. I remember my father saying he had a young brother who went out to Canada and the family lost track of him completely. This Murray might possibly be a son."

"But wouldn't his name be Elliot Murray?" asked Patty.

"He could have dropped the Elliot," explained the Colonel. "There's no hyphen so he could have done it quite easily if he had wanted to—and he might have wanted to for all sorts of reasons. Elliot Murray is a bit of a mouthful and an awful nuisance if you have to sign a lot of papers, I can tell you that."

Will was about to suggest to the Colonel that he ought to be careful, but remembering that he had said these words already, with regard to money matters, he decided to refrain. People who keep on advising one to be careful are apt to be a bit boring.

"Oh do, Daddy!" cried Patty. "Write and ask him —or something. It would be fun."

"You seem very keen on having another cousin," said Colonel Elliot Murray smiling.

"Cousins are nice," declared Patty with conviction.

3

Soon after lunch Will and Patty made their escape to the garden, where they could chat in peace. It had always been a wild sort of garden—a paradise for children who enjoyed climbing trees and playing hide-and-seek —but now it was wilder than ever; the bushes and trees had been allowed to grow unchecked, in fact it had become a positive jungle.

"Daddy doesn't care and Mummy doesn't notice," said Patty with a heavy sigh. She hesitated and then added in a low voice, "Mummy was talking to you about Rae."

"Yes," said Will uncomfortably. "Yes—she was."

"I knew," nodded Patty. "There's a sort of look in

her eyes when she's been talking about him. It frightens me."

" Surely it would be better to tell her——" began Will.

" Oh, we have—often. The doctor tried to tell her but she didn't take it in. She doesn't seem able to understand."

" She understands other things."

" I know. Sometimes I think she really knows that he won't come back—ever. I mean she knows inside herself but won't let herself believe it."

" But why, Patty? "

" Because she couldn't bear it. That's why."

" I don't understand what you mean."

" It's a sort of Bluebeard's Chamber. She knows there's something dreadful inside so she won't open the door."

" You're making it sound like a nightmare! "

" It is a nightmare," said Patty with a shudder. " If the door opens what will happen? It might kill her—or —or worse."

There was a little silence and then Patty added, " It's so awful for Daddy. That's what's wearing him down."

They talked about other things after that, remembering old times and renewing the bond between them. Patty had always been like a sister and she still was. It was a very comfortable sort of relationship—you could say what you liked to Patty and she understood. Will had met lots of girls in his wanderings but there was always " a sort of nonsense " about them. You could tease them and laugh with them; you could even flirt with them a little; but you could never talk to them comfortably and easily like this.

" You're just the same, Patty," said Will suddenly.

" So are you," declared Patty, smiling at him.

They had said this before, of course—in slightly different words—but there was no harm in saying it again.

Chapter 4

AFTER A week Will had settled down so completely that he felt as if he had never been away. His years among " unknown men " seemed like a dream. Broadmeadows was his home and these people were his people—to converse with them was like pulling on an old comfortable pair of shoes. He found himself dropping into words and phrases which he had known long ago. (They would have resented anything in the nature of a " put-on accent," but there was no fear of that. Will knew them too well.) For instance, one morning when he happened to be in the tiny potting-shed and old MacLaggan appeared at the door, he found himself saying, " Are you wanting in? " and saying it quite naturally. Thinking this over afterwards, Will decided that the English translation (which was obviously " Do you want to come in? ") did not really mean the same—and of course it was not nearly so friendly!

Having dug himself in, Will sounded his father about trying modern methods of management, and discovered that Mr. Hastie was quite willing to co-operate and to spend money upon modern equipment for the farms.

" Do what you like, Will," he said. " Don't go too fast, that's all. Look about and talk to people and make sure that the new methods are better than the old ones before you chuck the old ones overboard. There's money to spend on the estate but we don't want to waste it."

This was good advice and Will took it. He talked to everybody. He went round all the farms in the neighbourhood—and beyond—and made copious notes. This kept him busy but all the same he managed to find time to visit Langford House two or three times a week. He had a standing invitation to " drop in " whenever he could, just as he had done in the old days.

One afternoon when Will dropped in he found nobody at home. He wandered round the house looking for Patty, and at last made up his mind to try the old playroom in the attic. So far he had avoided the old playroom—there were too many memories—but he wanted to see Patty and she might be there. He mounted the steep wooden stairs—which still creaked noisily in the same places—and pushed open the door.

The room was empty and tidy but obviously it was used, not abandoned as Will had feared. Patty was the only person likely to use it so probably she came up here when she felt in need of peace—when she wanted to be alone.

Will looked around and saw that nothing had been changed. Except for the tidiness it was just as he remembered. The shelves were crowded with books of all kinds and in various stages of dilapidation. The squirrel which had been stuffed and set up by Rae still stood upon its bracket in the glass case . . . and the case was slightly chipped at the corner. Will himself was responsible for the chip, it had happened when he was practising a golf swing. The dart-board hung upon the wall; the fishing-rods were stacked in the corner. There was a darn in the middle of the carpet where it had been burned when the spirit-lamp upset. Will and Rae had been brewing up various chemicals—it was a scientific experiment—and the whole thing had exploded and burned the carpet. Patty had mended it of course (you could always depend upon Patty to cover up your crimes), but the darn in slightly different-coloured wool was plainly visible if you knew where to look.

The room was so full of Rae's belongings that it almost seemed as if Rae were there in person. The big basket chair by the window in which Rae had sprawled and talked and read was moulded by his body. Will could almost see him sitting there with his long legs blocking the floor space. If Rae were reading and you wanted to pull down the blind or to shut or open the window you had to step over yards of legs and ankles. Rae seldom noticed what you were doing, he had an amazing power of concentration, but you had to be careful for sometimes he noticed at the last minute and moved his feet. . . .

In this room Will and Rae had swapped stamps and practised conjuring tricks; they had played card-games on wet afternoons; they had made toffee and tied flies . . . and how they had talked! They had talked about school, they had discussed religion; sometimes they had talked sense, but more often absolute nonsense. They had quarrelled and made it up and become closer friends than before.

Theirs was a real true friendship, based on solid rock. They had shared everything, from pet rabbits to a small but efficient camera and a developing tank to which both had contributed all their Christmas tips. For a time they had been mad on photography—the results of this craze were framed in *passe-partout* by Patty's neat fingers; many of them were still to be seen hanging on the walls.

One craze had followed another; most of the crazes they had shared, but there was one craze peculiar to Will, which Rae had neither shared nor understood. The craze for dancing had taken Will at the beginning of the Christmas holidays before the war. He was seventeen and Rae was nineteen, Patty was sixteen and considered herself " grown-up." Like most girls of her age, Patty adored parties and was delighted to have Will as an escort for it was much more fun to go to parties with somebody who liked dancing instead of with a reluctant brother who hung about the door and kept on asking if she would like to go home.

Will remembered one occasion when he had called for Patty and found Rae in the play-room cleaning his gun.

" Patty will be ready in a minute," said Rae. " Hand me the oil. It's just behind you on the chimney-piece . . . or no, perhaps I'd better get it myself. You'll make a mess of your hands."

Will had no intention of handing him the oil—so that was all right.

" Can't think why you *like* it," grumbled Rae. " Dressing up like a tailor's dummy and hopping round the room with a lot of girls! "

" I like dancing with girls," said Will rather sheepishly.

" Why? "

" I don't know, exactly. I just—like it—that's all."

" Rather you than me! " He glanced at Will and

43

added with a little smile, " You look very nice, I must admit. I expect the girls enjoy dancing with you. No lack of partners? "

Will did not answer the jibe. Instead he said, " You don't like girls, do you? "

" It isn't so much that I don't like them. I'm just not interested in them. Flimsy creatures," said Rae, holding up the gun and squinting through the barrels. " Flimsy and frilly, with fuzzy hair and powder on their noses and red stuff on their mouths."

" Patty isn't—hasn't, I mean."

" Oh Patty's different," declared her brother. "Patty isn't like a girl at all."

Will was silent. He could not agree but it was difficult to put his reason into words. He was still searching for words when the door opened and Patty appeared; dressed for the occasion in a new frock. (In Will's opinion Patty " looked like a girl " and a very pretty one at that.)

" How do you like me? " she cried, whizzing round the room on the tips of her toes.

" Oh, you're all right," said Rae reluctantly. " But as a matter of fact I like you a lot better in your tweeds . . . and if you take my advice you won't let the parents see you with that red stuff on your mouth."

2

It was queer that Will should remember the little scene so clearly after all these years. They had left Rae cleaning his gun and had crept down the back stairs like a couple of conspirators so that the parents might

not see the red stuff on Patty's mouth, but he could
not remember the dance at all, which seemed even
queerer.

Rae was an excellent shot—much better than Will—
he had started shooting with a small gun specially made
to fit him and given to him by his father on his twelfth
birthday. When Rae outgrew the gun and was promoted
to a man-size weapon he hung up the little gun on the
wall above the chimney-piece. It was still there. For
some reason it had often slipped sideways and hung
crookedly upon its hooks and this annoyed Rae; he had
straightened it dozens of times saying as he did so, " It's
because they *dust* it—or something. Why can't they
leave it alone?" The gun was crooked now, Will
noticed, so he went over to the chimney-piece and put it
straight . . . and then he hesitated and wondered how
long it was since it had been cleaned.

I had better have a look at the gun, thought Will.

Yes, it was just as he had feared. There were tiny
specks of rust in both barrels. Fortunately no serious
damage had occurred but quite definitely it needed to
be cleaned and re-oiled. Will found the cleaning
materials, the oil and the pull-through, in the usual
place and started upon his task.

The little gun was in pieces upon the table when
Patty came in.

" Hallo! " she exclaimed. " I saw your car in the
drive and wondered where you'd got to . . . Oh, you're
cleaning the little gun! "

" I thought it might need cleaning—and it did."

" Oh dear, I should have thought of that! "

" You've got a lot to do. It was crooked, so I put it

straight and then I decided to have a look at it—that's all."

There was no need to say more for of course Patty remembered—and of course Will knew she remembered. What a lot of memories they shared! He hoped Patty would not thank him for cleaning the little gun (it would have hurt him to be thanked, for it would have put him outside the fence), but it never occurred to Patty to thank him. She had gone across to the window and was standing there looking out. It had started to rain heavily—silver rods of rain were falling and the drops were chasing each other down the pane. She stood there for a long time without speaking. She was fiddling with the cord of the blind. (Will remembered that she had always done that when she was upset or miserable—and he remembered how the habit had annoyed Rae. He remembered Rae saying in his big-brotherly voice, "For goodness sake, Patty, leave the blind alone. Some day when you're least expecting it you'll bring the whole contraption down on your head. That's what'll happen—mark my words.")

The silence continued for so long that at last it became unbearable.

"Patty, what are you thinking about?" asked Will.

"Rae, of course," she replied. "I think of him a lot—especially here, and especially lately. Sometimes it seems as if . . ." She hesitated.

"As if what?"

She said, "I did sort of—forget, but seeing you has brought him back again. It's as if he were here with us —the three of us."

"I've felt that too."

46

" I'd like to tell you something, Will. It's a thing that has worried me a lot. It has worried me off and on ever since Rae was killed. I've never told anybody about it, not anybody at all. He said not to—so I didn't— but I don't think he would mind me telling you. Rae always shared everything with you. Perhaps it wasn't important, but—but it may have been. We shall never know now——"

" Patty, what are you trying to say? "

She did not answer but went over to the old shabby desk and unlocked a drawer and took out a letter. For a moment she hesitated with it in her hand and then held it out to Will.

" I'm to read it? " asked Will.

She nodded.

He unfolded the thin sheet of paper. The letter was an untidy pencil scrawl in Rae's big bold writing:

Leave at last, Patty dear! Perhaps I'll be home before this letter—you never know. How I've been longing for a spot of leave! All the more because I've got something to tell you. I haven't said anything about it because I want to explain the whole thing. Don't say anything to anybody and especially don't say anything to the parents. It might worry them a bit. There's nothing to worry about but you know how they worry about nothing. I'll explain everything when I come. No time for more but lots of love.

Rae.

Will raised his eyes and looked at her.

" It came after we heard he had been killed," explained

Patty. " I didn't show it to them—what was the use?
Besides, I knew it would only upset them—and—and
he said not to—but I thought and thought and thought
. . ." She was in tears now.

" Oh, Patty! " Will exclaimed in distress.

" What could it—have been? " she whispered. " Do
you think it could have been—something important? "

" You've no clue at all? "

" Nothing. Oh, Will, doesn't it seem dreadful?
I mean—not to know—what it was."

Will's one idea was to comfort her. He said, " Perhaps
it wasn't important, or at least not all that important.
He dashed it off in a hurry—you can see that. Could it
have been his M.C.? You only heard about that afterwards, didn't you? "

" I thought of that, but why should they worry
because he had won the M.C.? Would that worry
them? "

" It might, you know. People don't pick up an M.C.
for nothing; it might have worried them to think of
him being in danger. I expect Rae wanted to tell them
about it himself; I can see him explaining it, playing
it down like anything and making a joke of it, can't
you? "

" Yes, but still——"

" That's what it was."

" But it really doesn't fit."

" It fits well enough for a man in a hurry."

" Do you think so? It doesn't—doesn't satisfy me,"
said Patty miserably. " I can't help feeling it was
something terribly important."

Will took up the letter and read it again, more care-

fully. He said, " I think you're making too much of it
—honestly I do. It was something nice—it was something he wanted to tell you."

" But why should the parents worry if it was something nice? "

" They worried about everything," said Will.

This was perfectly true. Will could remember half
a dozen instances with which to substantiate his point.
He remembered the day when Rae fell off the pony and
bumped his head on a stone. For a few moments he
lay upon the ground unconscious and then sat up and
exclaimed, " For goodness' sake don't tell the parents!"

" You remember? " asked Will.

" Yes, of course. It was frightful, wasn't it? I thought
Rae was dead."

" Yes," agreed Will. " Yes, it was frightful—but
you see what I mean, don't you, Patty? "

" You mean we always spared them."

" Exactly. You were always saying not to tell the
parents."

Patty nodded. " Rae hated them to worry——"

" Well, there you are," said Will. " It was either his
M.C. or else some small thing—a mere nothing—but
Rae didn't want them to worry. He was going to explain
it to them when he got home."

" Yes," said Patty, but she said it doubtfully.

" Do you really know nothing else at all? " pursued
Will. " I mean didn't Rae's colonel write to you at
the time? "

" He was killed—several of the other officers were
killed, too. It was a bomb," explained Patty in a low
voice. " Daddy wrote to the farmer near Badlieu. Rae

49

had been billeted at his farm. His name was Jean Leyrisse. We didn't know what else to do. We were all —sort of—stunned——"

" Didn't the farmer reply to the letter? "

Patty shook her head. " We didn't know what else to do," she repeated helplessly.

Will did not see what else they could have done— and at any rate it was too late now to do anything to clear up the mystery—but he went on talking quietly and sensibly, trying to comfort Patty and to ease her mind. At last he managed to convince her that the letter she had received from Rae could not have meant anything important—but the odd thing was he convinced Patty without convincing himself.

As he took the road home through Torfoot he thought about it—and wondered. He was glad he had convinced Patty, for what was the use of Patty making herself miserable over a hint in a letter which had been written more than ten years ago—a letter dashed off by a man in a hurry, a man who half expected to be home before the letter was received? Yes, he was glad he had convinced Patty. Perhaps she would stop thinking about it now.

Chapter 5

IT WAS a Saturday, and by this time it had become
customary for Will to ride over to Langford every
Saturday morning and stay to lunch, so when Will rose
from the breakfast table Mr. Hastie looked up and said,
" You might take that book about heaths. The Colonel
wanted to see it; I left it on the hall-table."

" Not to-day," said Will uncomfortably. " I mean
I'm not going to Langford to-day—unless you specially
want me to take the book."

" No hurry at all. It will do just as well to-morrow.
You'll be going to-morrow, I suppose."

" Er—no—not to-morrow——"

" Not to-morrow!" exclaimed Mr. Hastie. "What's
happened, Will? You haven't fallen out with Patty,
have you? "

" Goodness, no! How could I possibly? I just thought
they might be getting a bit tired of me going over so
often—and of course the cousin is there now, so—
so——"

" Hugo Elliot Murray? "

" Yes, he's there for ten days."

" What's that got to do with it? "

" Well—Patty's engaged to him, so I thought——"

" Not engaged to marry him? "

Will nodded.

" Good heavens! " exclaimed Mr. Hastie in dismay.

" Don't you like him? " asked Will. " I thought everybody liked him—and of course he's the heir—so it's all very suitable and—and convenient."

" Far too suitable and convenient. Oh, he's a nice enough fellow," admitted Mr. Hastie. " I've nothing against him except that he talks a bit too much. I don't mean he throws his weight about or anything like that ... all the same I hope they haven't pushed Patty into it."

" Pushed Patty into it! " cried Will. " You mean because he's the heir? Oh no, Patty wouldn't! You don't know Patty if you think——"

" Not for herself," agreed Mr. Hastie. " And of course she wouldn't dream of marrying anybody she wasn't fond of, but it's possible to deceive oneself, you know. It's possible to get pushed into things—gently pushed. I've no right to say so but to my mind it seems —well, it seems too suitable and convenient. That's all."

Will had thought this himself but he had changed his mind. He said, " You wouldn't think so if you had seen her yesterday. I met her in Torfoot and she was full of excitement at the prospect of Hugo's arrival."

" H'm! " said Mr. Hastie and buried himself in *The Scotsman.*

For a few moments Will hesitated; he would have liked to know a bit more about " Hugo," but it was difficult to frame his questions and obviously his father considered the conversation at an end.

Will wandered out to the stable to look at Duffer and to give him a piece of apple. Every morning Will had gone to see Duffer with an apple in his pocket and every morning Duffer had eaten it without the slightest sign of appreciation. He would have eaten anything that was offered to him, thought Will in disgust.

Habits are quickly formed so it seemed strange not to be going over to Langford, it seemed that there was nothing much to do. He could go for a ride, of course, thought Will, hesitating. There was no real pleasure in riding Duffer, but it was better than hanging about—and moping—so Duffer was saddled and bridled and Will set out for an aimless ride. He rode up the hill through the woods, taking the same path as he had taken the first day after his return. It had been early spring then—a time of promise—with tender green leaves on the old trees and primroses in the sheltered hollows; now it was high summer and the foliage on the oaks and beeches was thick and heavy. The birds had been singing then; now they were mute. Will's thoughts were different too.

Presently he came to the rocky mound from which Langford could be seen. He had not climbed it since his return, but to-day, on a sudden impulse, he tied Duffer to a tree and scrambled up. The trees had grown a bit since the old days but the long grey house by the river was still visible, drowsing peacefully in the morning sunshine. Its rows of windows glittered and, high up beneath the grey slate roof, was the play-room window with the scarlet blind.

Will wondered whether the room was being used. Perhaps Patty and Hugo sat there and chatted when they wanted to be alone. It would be a safe retreat. But certainly they were not there this morning for the blind was half-way down. He realised that it was just an accident (somebody had drawn it down and nobody had bothered to draw it up again) but there it was, half-mast, which had always meant that Rae and Patty would be going out and any plans they had made with Will were cancelled. No use coming, said the blind.

Long ago Will had been exiled from Langford—it had been mumps in those days, now it was Hugo!—but it came to the same thing. (Will smiled ruefully at the ridiculous idea.) There were differences, of course. For instance, he was not really exiled to-day, for if he liked he could ride down to the river and cross the ford and lunch at Langford. No doubt they would be quite pleased to see him . . . but it would be no pleasure to sit through lunch and watch Hugo and Patty looking at each other, to listen to Hugo talking.

Will sat upon the topmost pinnacle of rock and looked at Langford; he felt absurdly like that child of nine years old who had sat there long ago. That child had possessed a little spy-glass, so he could see a good deal more of what went on at Langford; the grown-up Will had to rely upon his own long-sighted eyes.

There was a large red-and-white-striped umbrella on the small lawn at one side of the house and, beneath it, a deck-chair with somebody reclining in it; Will could not see who it was (in fact he could only see two long legs in grey slacks) but he was pretty certain it was " Hugo." Presently a figure emerged from the house with a tray, and although it was too far off to recognise the figure he knew it was Patty because she was wearing a cherry-coloured cardigan.

Patty put the tray beside the chair and after a short

conversation she returned to the house. The incident annoyed Will. Why should Patty bring the man a drink —or whatever it was? And why didn't the man get up when he saw her coming?

Will continued to sit on his look-out tower for some time, but nothing else happened (nobody came out of the house and nobody went in), so presently he scrambled down and untied the patient Duffer and rode home.

2

" Rae is late, isn't he? " said Mrs. Elliot Murray. " The mince will be cold if he doesn't come soon. We had better put some on a plate and ask Teena to keep it hot in the oven for him."

" Rae isn't coming, darling," said Patty quickly.

" But they've laid his place——"

" That was for Will," explained Patty. " Will usually comes on a Saturday. You know that, don't you, Mummy? "

" Who is Will? " asked Hugo. " I haven't met him, have I? "

Patty had risen and was clearing away the knives and forks and removing the empty chair.

" Did Will say he wasn't coming? " asked Colonel Elliot Murray.

" No, not really," replied Patty. " But it doesn't matter. I mean he comes if he can. Something must have prevented him—perhaps he'll come to-morrow instead."

" Who is Will? " repeated Hugo.

" Will Hastie—they're our nearest neighbours,"

replied the Colonel, and went on to explain that Will had been serving abroad but had now retired and was living with his father at Broadmeadows. " He's a thoroughly good fellow," added the Colonel. " You'll like Will immensely. We're all very fond of Will."

" In that case I'm sure to like him," said Hugo without enthusiasm.

Hugo had arrived at Langford the night before and having driven all the way from Wiltshire he was quite pleased to spend an idle morning sitting in the garden while Patty was busy in the house. But now he felt rested and ready for anything so when Patty suggested they should go for a walk together Hugo was all for it.

" We'll walk over to Peacehaven," said Patty. " I want to see Brenda Heston about Guides—we could drop in to tea. The Hestons like people ' dropping in ' so they'll be pleased to see us. It will be killing two birds with one stone. You don't mind, do you? "

" Why should I mind? " asked Hugo. " And why is the house called Peacehaven? What a ghastly name! "

" It doesn't fit very well," agreed Patty. " But the poor Hestons built it near Torfoot because they wanted peace and quiet . . ." and she explained about the raging, roaring jets which had rendered the poor Hestons' previous abode intolerable.

Patty said no more than the truth when she agreed that the name chosen by the Hestons did not fit. It was a strange name to find cheek by jowl with Langford and Mosslands and Burncrook and Auchenbeck and Craigrowan—and all the rest. The house itself was every bit as strange as its name and occasioned a great deal of controversy in the district, for although it was a pleasant enough erection (there was nothing ugly about it) it was as out of place as a bird of paradise in a hen run. There it stood upon a slight rise in the ground so that you could see it for miles—you could not help seeing it—with its red-tiled roof and its cream-coloured walls and its large modern windows flashing in the sunshine.

"It's an eyesore," declared Mrs. Hunter Brown of Mosslands. "That's what it is. Anybody who could build a place like that must be frightful. I don't want to know them."

Her friends agreed (most people agreed with Mrs. Hunter Brown), but soon curiosity overcame repulsion and various ladies in the district went to call. Mrs. Heston welcomed them warmly, for she found it dull at Torfoot; she gave her visitors an excellent tea and showed them all over the house—which was exactly what they wanted.

The inside of the house was modern and labour-saving. Everything in it was absolutely new. The ladies from Craigrowan and Burncrook, from Dunmore and Auchenbeck and Mosslands looked about them with awe. They looked at the kitchen with its built-in sinks and cupboards and the electric mixer and the electric potato-peeler and the deep-freeze machine and the washing-machine which washed up dishes or clothes—and dried them as well. They saw the hatch which opened straight into the dining-room (and thought of their own enormous kitchens with the stone floors and the long passage which led to the dining-room and had to be scrubbed at least twice weekly by the woman who came in from the village to oblige). They looked at the brightly painted bathrooms, with the built-in baths;

they admired the central heating which was run by oil and could be turned on or off—as the case might be—by touching a switch in the hall. They saw the electric fires, which looked like real fires—or very nearly—and agreed that they must save a tremendous amount of labour. They looked at the carpets, all fitted of course (and thought of the shabby rugs on their own wooden floors); they praised the fitted-in wardrobes and the mirrors which hung upon swivels so that you could see yourself back and front and sideways. They sat upon the brand-new sofas and the chairs which supported your back in exactly the right place. Then they went home and told their husbands all about it. They stirred up the logs upon the open hearth—piled up with ashes—sank into the large shabby chair with the sagging springs, and sighed. " It's marvellous," they declared. " It's simply incredible—but I wouldn't live in a house like that for a fortune. I don't know why, really. There's every comfort, but somehow it isn't—comfortable."

" It has no soul," said Mrs. Hunter Brown.

Patty told Hugo all this as they walked along, and made him laugh.

" And what about the lady from Langford? " he inquired. " Does she approve of built-in cupboards or does she prefer a house with a soul? "

Patty smiled at him and said, " But you could have both, couldn't you? Not all of it of course—but some of the labour-saving things would be possible even at Langford. I shall screw them out of Daddy one at a time. You'll see."

" Patty, you're a darling," declared Hugo. " When we're married you won't need to screw things out of me;

you shall have everything I can afford to give you. Patty, why shouldn't we be married soon? It's hateful only seeing you for a few days now and then. Let's fix a date, shall we? "

" How can we? You know we can't, Hugo. I can't leave the parents and there's your mother to consider. She wouldn't like it at all."

" Mother wouldn't mind. In fact it was Mother's suggestion."

" But you said——"

" Yes, I know. You see I thought Mother would be unhappy at the thought of leaving Bellstead, but of course there's no need for her to go away. It's a big house and she could easily have her own rooms without interfering with us in the least. It's a grand idea, isn't it? "

Patty agreed somewhat tepidly.

" You get on splendidly with Mother," Hugo pointed out.

" Yes of course," said Patty. " But I couldn't——"

"Bellstead is getting a bit too much for Mother," continued Hugo. " She isn't as young as she was and you could take a lot off her shoulders. I'm sure it would work out well."

" Hugo, I couldn't! I simply couldn't go away and leave the parents. It's impossible! "

" You must some day, darling. We can't wait for ever."

Patty did not reply. She was suddenly breathless.

" Patty, please say yes. It would make me so happy. I want you at Bellstead. I want you all the time instead of just for a week every now and then——"

" But what would they do without me! "

" We could get someone else to look after them. As a matter of fact your mother needs a trained nurse— someone who would know exactly how to manage her."

" She doesn't really," declared Patty. " I can manage her perfectly well; she isn't a bit difficult to manage; you don't understand her, that's all . . . and anyway it isn't *her* that I'm worrying about. It's Daddy."

Hugo was silent for a few moments and then he said, " Patty, what are you waiting for? Tell me that."

She could not tell him what they were waiting for. She had not faced the future even in her own mind— not really faced it—so how could she put it into words?

" Six months," said Hugo, slipping his hand through her arm and giving it a little squeeze. " I could wait six months. It's the uncertainty that's getting me down. We could look about and find someone to take your place."

" Nobody could take my place."

" I didn't mean that, exactly," said Hugo quickly. " Of course nobody could take your place. I just meant someone who could look after them."

" Nobody could," repeated Patty. " Oh of course lots of people could do what I do in the house, but nobody could be what I am—to Daddy."

Hugo sighed. " Well, what's going to happen? When will you be free? Are we to go on waiting indefinitely? "

Patty did not answer. There was only one way in which she would be free—and she could not bear to think of it.

" Please, Patty——" began Hugo.

" No, no! " she cried. " I couldn't! I don't want to!

I love them dearly. They would be miserable—and I would be miserable too!"

"What about me being miserable?"

"But you aren't miserable—not really—are you Hugo?"

She turned her head to face him and she looked so sweet with a wan little smile shining through her tears that Hugo's heart was melted.

"Not to worry," he said. "Not to worry, darling. We'll just—leave it. You've promised to marry me sooner or later—that's the main thing—and perhaps something may turn up. You never know what's waiting for you round the corner."

They had stopped for a few minutes while they were talking but now they walked on. The conversation was over. Patty told herself that nothing had happened; everything was just as it had been before; some day in the far-off future she would marry Hugo. He had said not to worry, so that was all right, wasn't it? But Patty did not feel very happy, for everything was not quite as it had been before, that was the trouble. Before, there had been obstacles on both sides—Hugo's mother and "the parents"—but now Hugo's obstacle had vanished, only her obstacles remained and of course her obstacles were insuperable. Did that mean she ought to release Hugo from their engagement, wondered Patty. Perhaps it did, perhaps she ought to suggest it. She decided to think it over seriously.

There was no time to think about it now, for already they had arrived at Peacehaven and were mounting the steps which led to the yellow front door.

3

The Hestons were out—all except Brenda, who was practising knots for the Girl Guide Meeting, due to take place that evening—but as it was really Brenda whom Patty wanted to see this was all to the good. She had said she wanted to talk about " Guides " which was true—people who are interested in Guides can talk about them till the cows come home—but there was another subject in which Patty was interested and upon which she wanted information. Hugo was bored with the " Guides " but he pricked up his ears when Patty moved on to the second subject.

" About those Murrays," said Patty. " I mean the man who was your father's partner, Brenda. What are they like? "

" They're very nice," replied Brenda. " Look, Patty, do tell me. Is this the way to make an anchor bend? "

" No, it isn't," declared Patty. " Oh, Brenda, do listen. I want to know about the Murrays. It's important."

Thus adjured, Brenda put aside the piece of string and gave all her attention to the District Commissioner —who, of course, was her boss.

" What do you want to know? " she inquired. " There's Mr. and Mrs. Murray and Duncan and Edna and Jane. The girls are very nice and very pretty —especially Edna."

" What about Duncan? "

" Oh he's very nice," replied Brenda (in a casual sort of voice, which did not deceive Patty in the least).

62

" Duncan has just been made a junior partner in the firm. It's nice, isn't it? I mean he's been hoping for that, so—so—it's nice."

" Very nice indeed," agreed Patty.

" Why do you want to know about them? " asked Hugo, hiding a yawn.

" Because they're relations," replied Patty. " At least Daddy thinks they may be. Mr. Murray is probably the son of Daddy's father's brother who went to Canada and got lost . . . and if they're my relations they're yours as well, Hugo, so you ought to be interested in them."

" Uncle Thomas ought to be careful——" began Hugo, but the girls were not listening.

" Oh, Patty, what fun! " exclaimed Brenda. " Mr. Murray was born in Canada, I know that. Duncan told me. Shall I write to Duncan and ask him all about it? "

" You had better not," said Hugo quickly. " I mean what's the good of it? We might not like them—and if anything is to be done it should be done through a lawyer. Personally I should leave it alone."

" But they're cousins, Hugo! " cried Patty.

" How do you know? There are thousands of Murrays in Canada—and even if they are cousins they aren't very near ones, are they? "

" Duncan would be my second cousin," said Patty in surprise. " That's *quite* near—and Brenda says he's nice. What more do you want? It isn't as if we had lots of cousins. You're the only one I've got."

Hugo said nothing, but it was obvious that he would prefer to remain Patty's only cousin.

Presently Mr. Heston appeared and after chatting for a few minutes and drinking a cup of tea he took Hugo to see the garden. So far the garden was not very spectacular but there were possibilities in the site and Hugo was always willing to give advice to those who were willing to take it. Sitting together by the window, the girls watched the two men strolling down the path; every now and then Hugo stopped and gesticulated.

" Hugo knows a lot about gardens," said Patty. She did not say it proudly, in fact she said it a trifle apologetically, or so Brenda thought. But Brenda adored Patty and her ear was attuned to every inflexion in her idol's voice. Brenda did not think Hugo was " nearly good enough for Patty "—perhaps she would not have thought anybody good enough.

" He knows a lot about all sorts of things," suggested Brenda.

" Yes," said Patty. She added, " Look here, Brenda, I'll show you now how to make an anchor bend."

Chapter 6

"Where is Will?" asked Colonel Elliot Murray. "I haven't seen him for days. What's become of the fellow?"

"I don't know," said Patty vaguely. "No, he hasn't been here for ages. Perhaps he's busy or something."

"Ask him over," said the Colonel. "Ask them both to come to dinner. It will be nice for Hugo and Will to meet each other and have a crack."

If Will had been asked alone he would have found some excuse, but Mr. Hastie was included in the invitation and saw no reason to refuse. He enjoyed a chat with Colonel Elliot Murray and they always gave you an extremely good dinner at Langford.

"I suppose Hugo will be there," said Mr. Hastie as they drove over to Langford together in the little car. "Have you met him yet?"

"No," said Will.

"Nice-looking chap," said Mr. Hastie. "But not good enough for Patty. Perhaps it's a bit unfair to say so, for I scarcely know him, but that's what I think."

Will remained silent. It was true that he had not met Hugo Elliot Murray but he had seen him and noticed that he was very good looking indeed—tall and fair and slender. In fact (thought Will) he was far too good looking. Fair hair was all very well, a chap couldn't help the colour of his hair, but if Hugo Elliot Murray had invested in a bottle of pomade he could have smoothed down those curls . . . or better still he could have told the barber to cut his hair a good deal shorter.

Will had seen Hugo Elliot Murray in the post-office at Torfoot—buying stamps—and had taken an instant dislike to the fellow. For one thing he was speaking far too loudly (Miss White was deaf, of course, but she was not as deaf as that), and for another his tweed jacket was nipped in at the waist. Who but an absolute cad would wear a jacket like that? Last but not least, when Hugo had completed his purchase he strode off gaily, jumped into the Langford car and drove away. The Langford car, mark you! The fellow had a car of his own; why use the Langford car to do his shopping?

Will had the better of Hugo in one respect, for Will had seen Hugo but Hugo had not seen Will—or at least Hugo had not known it was Will Hastie who stood beside him at the counter. Will had known it was Hugo Elliot Murray because by this time he knew everybody in Torfoot, and seeing a tall stranger (with a revolting jacket) he had known at once that it could be none other than the heir of Langford.

All this went through Will's head as he drove his father over to dinner at Langford, so it is not surprising that his father found him very poor company.

Dinner went off reasonably well. The Colonel had insisted that his old friend should sit beside him, so Mr. Hastie was pleased. Hugo was in good form and chatted pleasantly. Patty kept the ball rolling, not saying a great deal herself but encouraging the others. Mrs. Elliot Murray was completely silent but she did not look unhappy as she sometimes did.

After dinner they all went into the drawing-room, except the two old gentlemen who were left behind to finish, and Patty having been persuaded to play the piano it was natural that Hugo should take up a position beside her to turn over the pages of her music. Will found himself paired off with his hostess and sat down near her by the fire. He had been frightened of her at first but now he understood her better and was able to talk to her simply and kindly as he would have talked to a child. To-night, when for some reason or other he was feeling wretched, no other companion would have suited him so well.

"How are you, Aunt Margaret?" he asked.

"Oh, I'm wonderfully well, dear. I'm afraid you have a headache, haven't you? I was watching you at dinner and I felt sure you had a headache. I have them often but I find a little aspirin does me good. Do you ever take aspirin?"

"No," said Will. "As a matter of fact I hardly ever——"

"And I get confused," said Mrs. Elliot Murray confidentially. "I get very confused sometimes—it's such a horrid feeling. I think if Rae could come home I should feel better. He hasn't been home for months —not since last Christmas, you know. I've noticed that Thomas and Patty don't like talking about Rae. I wonder why. Do you think he can be ill?"

"No, I'm sure he's not ill," said Will gently.

She sighed. " That's all right then," she said. " As long as he isn't ill . . ."

Hugo was singing now and Patty was playing his accompaniment.

" That man has a good voice," whispered Mrs. Elliot Murray. " It's a tenor, of course. I like a baritone better."

" So do I," agreed Will. " A baritone is much more pleasant."

" Still, he can't help it, can he? "

" He could help singing," said Will. " If I had a voice like that I wouldn't sing at all—not even in my bath."

Will had not expected his companion to understand the joke so he was not disappointed when she changed the subject.

" Patty is going to marry him," she said. " Do you think it's all right, Will? "

" All right? " echoed Will in surprise.

" I don't care for him very much. He never talks to me like you do, so I never get to know him any better. Do you think he's nice enough for Patty? "

" No," said Will.

" Oh dear," she said sadly. " Thomas thinks he's nice but Thomas is so easily taken in."

It was true, thought Will. Colonel Elliot Murray was the sort of man who always thinks the best of his fellow creatures; he was always ready to listen to a " hard-luck story." Sometimes the " hard-luck story " would be true and sometimes not but the Colonel always believed it implicitly.

" It's because he's so good and kind himself," added his wife.

68

"I know," Will agreed.

"We should have waited."

"Waited?"

"Yes, I said so at the time. We should have waited for Rae to come home before we allowed them to be engaged."

"They seem to—to be very fond of each other," said Will, glancing towards the piano where the two heads, one brown and one golden, were very close together, poring over a book of songs.

"I don't think so, dear. They think they're very fond of each other—but that's different, isn't it?"

Will hesitated. It was so queer talking to "Aunt Margaret." You never quite knew where you were. Sometimes she said the maddest things, like the White Queen in *Alice Through the Looking-Glass*, and sometimes she had moments of lucidity and was perfectly sane—though perhaps "sane" was not the right word, thought Will, glancing at her in perplexity. He thought of "fey," but that did not suit her either. It was as if she spent most of her time groping in a fog and then suddenly the fog cleared and she saw things more clearly than other people.

"Patty is like Thomas—easily taken in," added Patty's mother sadly.

"Yes," said Will. "But—but he isn't like a stranger. I mean you know who he is and all about him."

"He's James's son—there, wasn't I clever to remember? I can always remember things better when I'm talking to you. James was very selfish, not like Thomas at all. He was very good looking, with fair curly hair, so his mother spoilt him dreadfully." She hesitated and

69

then said, " But I meant to tell you something else. What was it, dear? "

" About Thomas and James? "

" Yes, they had a dreadful quarrel, you know. They didn't speak to each other for years—and then they made it up. That was quite right of course because brothers should forgive each other—it says so in the Bible—but there was no need to ask Hugo to come to Langford. Thomas keeps on asking him to come and he takes Hugo's advice about all sorts of things connected with the estate. I wonder why." She sighed and added, " Thomas doesn't tell me things now."

" He doesn't want to worry you, Aunt Margaret."

" You're a kind boy," she declared, smiling at him. " You always were kind and considerate. Ellen is kind, too. You remember Ellen, don't you? "

Will nodded. He had been at Langford so much in the old days that he knew all the Elliot Murray relations as well as his own. " Miss Ellen," as he called her, was the Colonel's sister; much younger than the Colonel and very lively and amusing. She had come quite often to stay at Langford and the children had loved her dearly and enjoyed her visits. Will remembered going for picnics with Miss Ellen; he could remember her sitting in front of the fire in the old play-room, roasting chestnuts or making toast for tea; he could remember her reading stories to them on wet afternoons. " Chief of our aunts," Rae had called her—half teasingly and half in earnest— and Miss Ellen had been pleased, as indeed she had every right to be. What was she like now, wondered Will. Somehow he could not imagine her " old."

" She's just the same," said Mrs. Elliot Murray

happily. "She's coming to stay—so you'll see her. Thomas has asked her to come."

"Where does she live?" asked Will. He regretted the words as soon as they were uttered for it was a mistake to ask Aunt Margaret a direct question. If one allowed her to talk in her own way she drifted along comfortably but questions confused her. The fog thickened.

"I—I don't remember——" she began. "Oh yes, of course—she lives at Bournemouth—with her mother. Old Mrs. Elliot Murray is a little blind so she couldn't manage without Ellen."

Old Mrs. Elliot Murray had been dead for years—as Will knew—and presumably was managing quite comfortably without her daughter, but Will left it alone. He would have liked to know where Miss Ellen was now and what she was doing, but it was useless to pursue the subject.

2

People who live in country places are inclined to keep "country hours" and shortly after ten o'clock the two Hasties were speeding home to Broadmeadows. Patty was half-way upstairs to bed when her father called her into his study.

"Just a moment," he said. "I want to talk to you, Patty."

He looked so grave that she was alarmed but she went in and sat on the hearth rug and began to blow up the embers of the fire. The Colonel sat down in his leather chair and watched her.

"Hugo has been talking to me," he said. "Perhaps

you can guess what it was about. He's right, you know. Long-drawn-out engagements are a mistake."

" But I couldn't leave you, Daddy! "

" Ellen would come."

" You mean come and live here always? "

" Yes, she would like it. I rang her up last night and she would sell the little house in Bournemouth and come back to Langford. It would really be coming home because, of course, she lived here when she was a child; she knows every stick and stone of the place. It's a good plan, isn't it? Your mother is very fond of Ellen."

" But wouldn't you miss me, Daddy? " asked Patty, gazing at him in amazement.

" My dear, I shall miss you dreadfully, but Ellen is very capable and kind—and to be quite honest it will be a relief to see you married before I die."

" You're not going to die! "

" Not yet awhile," he agreed, smiling. " But I'm getting on, you know, and I'd like to see you settled. Hugo is thoroughly sound. He's a very good fellow and you're very fond of each other so what's the use of waiting? "

She did not reply.

" What are you waiting for, Patty? "

It was the question Hugo had asked. " I don't know," said Patty in a very low voice—and then she laid her hand on her father's knee and exclaimed, " Yes, I *do* know! I don't want to leave you, Daddy."

" But you'll have to, sooner or later, my lamb. You can't expect Hugo to wait on indefinitely. It isn't fair. You see that, don't you? "

Patty had seen that before.

" I want to see you safe," added the Colonel with a sigh.

" Safe? "

" Yes, safely married to a first-rate fellow, a man who will take care of you when I'm no longer here——"

" But, Daddy——"

" And Hugo is the man for the job," declared the Colonel, patting her hand reassuringly. " Hugo is the man. We're agreed on that, aren't we? "

" Yes," said Patty. " Yes, Hugo and I—are—arc—very fond of each other—so—so if you really think——"

" That's right. You fix it up, my dear." He rose and stretched himself rather wearily. " Bed-time," he said.

The conversation was at an end. It had been quite a short conversation but full of unsaid words, for on both sides there were so many things which could not be mentioned.

Patty knew that her father was becoming more frail every day. He always seemed tired—he was tired of life, she thought—perhaps it was because he had nothing to live for. There was nothing for him to do; he had become too frail to manage his own property (the farms had been leased to tenants); he could neither shoot nor fish nor indulge in any other outdoor activities; he had never been fond of reading and there was seldom anything on television that amused him. Patty knew that he loved her dearly and was interested in all her doings and she made a point of finding little bits of local news and gossip to tell him, but apparently he thought he could do without her quite easily! She wondered if he really could. She had a feeling that if she lost her grip of him he would drift out of life slowly and gently and she would never see him again.

On Colonel Elliot Murray's side there were several things which could not be mentioned. He could not tell Patty to take Hugo while she could get him because if she kept him dangling he might get tired of waiting and find somebody else. He could not tell Patty that his greatest desire was that she should come back to Langford as its mistress, after he was dead, so that her children should be Elliot Murrays of Langford, and his grandson should inherit the old family home.

If Colonel Elliot Murray had been a different kind of man, less delicately minded, he might have mentioned these things to Patty, but being himself he could not even hint at them.

Chapter 7

THE WEDDING was arranged to take place after Christmas.
Hugo would have liked it to be sooner, but there was a
lot to be done. His mother was making plans for alterations at Bellstead so that she could have her own suite
of rooms and not interfere with her future daughter-in-
law. Miss Elliot Murray wanted time to sell her little
house at Bournemouth before coming north and Patty
declared that, what with one thing and another, she
could not be ready to leave Langford for at least six
months.

" There's no hurry," declared Patty. " After Christmas will be best."

Hugo was obliged to agree. It was something to
have got a date fixed. Meanwhile he decided to prolong
his visit to Langford. He had spent so little time in the
district that he knew very few of the neighbours but
now he saw that it would be a good thing to get to know
them; evidently the neighbours had the same idea for
he and Patty received quite a number of invitations.
They went to lunch at Craigrowan and to tea at Burncrook; Mrs. Hunter Brown of Mosslands gave a nice
party for them to which she invited everybody she could
think of. Naturally the Hasties were included.

The card arrived at Broadmeadows at breakfast.

"You'll go, of course," said Mr. Hastie, passing it across the table to his son. "You like these social occasions, don't you?"

"Too busy," declared Will.

"But, Will——"

"Why don't you go?" suggested Will.

"Not me!" Mr. Hastie exclaimed. "These parties aren't my line at all—they're crowded and noisy. You can't speak to the people you want to speak to, and even if you meet them in the crush you can't hear what they say—but you had better go. You like them."

"I'll write and say we can't manage it."

"Patty will be there——"

"Yes—and Hugo," agreed Will in disgust. "The party is obviously given in honour of the future Laird of Langford."

Mr. Hastie sighed, "It's a pity you dislike him so much, Will. Some day he'll be your neighbour. Could you not——"

"No, I can't stand him!"

There was a little silence after that.

"Why don't you take a holiday?" said Mr. Hastie suddenly. "Go off on your own for a fortnight."

"I might——" said Will. He hesitated and then added, "As a matter of fact I've been thinking about it. I'd like to go for a walking-tour in France."

"It would be hot."

"I don't mind," declared Will. "I wouldn't hurry—just saunter along at my own pace and see the country."

This was not Mr. Hastie's idea of a pleasant holiday; he said, "Take the car. I can get on perfectly well without it."

" Oh, thank you! It's very good of you but I'd rather hike," replied Will. " It's more fun, really. Are you sure you don't mind me going? You won't find it dull? "

" Don't worry about me. I'd like a postcard now and then just to know where you are and what you're doing. That's all."

The thing was settled just like that, for the Hasties knew each other so well that they did not waste words. He's an awfully decent old boy, thought Will, looking at his father affectionately . . . and Mr. Hastie, glancing at his son, said to himself; it will do the lad a world of good to shake a loose leg.

2

Mrs. Hunter Brown was surprised and disappointed when she received Will's polite refusal of her invitation. She had not expected old William to come to her party but she had been depending upon young Will. She rang him up and tried to persuade him to come, but he was not to be persuaded.

" I'm going away on Friday for a fortnight's holiday," he explained.

" But my party is on Thursday! "

" I know, but I'll be too busy. I'm terribly sorry but you know how it is when you're going away . . . all sorts of things to be done."

" That's just a fribble! "

" No, it isn't—really."

" Oh well, come and see me when you get home. Come and tell me all your adventures."

Will laughed and said he would. As a matter of fact he liked Mrs. Hunter Brown. She was not everybody's cup of tea. She was too forthright to be really popular —she said what she thought without fear or favour— and many of her neighbours found her alarming.

In spite of this, however, there were very few absentees from the party at Mosslands and when Patty and Hugo arrived the large, beautifully proportioned drawing-room was full of guests—all chattering. Mrs. Hunter Brown surged towards them like a battleship.

" You're late! " she exclaimed accusingly.

" I know," agreed Patty. " I'm awfully sorry. We were delayed."

This was not quite true. The fact was Hugo had refused point-blank to come to the party at six o'clock— the hour stated in the invitation—for he was not used to country ways. He had explained to Patty that if you were asked to a party at six o'clock the correct procedure was to roll up about seven.

" Well, never mind," said Mrs. Hunter Brown. " You're here, anyway. I was afraid you weren't coming. Everybody wants to meet Captain Elliot Murray."

" Everybody? " asked Hugo, looking around the room in surprise.

" Yes, of course," declared his hostess. " Come on, you'd better get it over. You aren't shy, are you? "

Fortunately Hugo was not shy.

3

Patty enjoyed parties and enjoyed Hugo's success in the social line. It was delightful to see him talking to

people—and winning golden opinions from the neighbours—but sometimes she wished she could have him
all to herself for a little. She was surprised and pleased
to discover that Hugo felt the same.

It was the day after the party when they were having
lunch at Langford that this discovery was made.

"What are you doing this afternoon?" inquired
Colonel Elliot Murray.

"Tea at Craigrowan," replied Patty.

"Oh help!" exclaimed Hugo. "Not another party!"

"I thought you liked parties——"

"So I do—but not every day. Couldn't we chuck it,
Patty?"

"I suppose we could," agreed Patty doubtfully.

"Why go if you don't want to?" asked Colonel Elliot
Murray. "You could ring up and explain. They
wouldn't mind, would they?"

Patty thought they would—but she was tempted.

"Let's chuck it," urged Hugo. "Let's go for a
picnic instead. You said we would climb that hill
together so why not do it this afternoon? It's far too
beautiful a day to waste at a stuffy tea-fight."

"Yes," agreed Patty. "Yes, we'll do it. This is the
very day for Cloudhill."

"Not Cloudhill!" exclaimed Colonel Elliot Murray
in alarm. "You're not thinking of climbing Cloudhill!"

"Oh, Daddy, what nonsense!" cried Patty. "There
isn't a cloud in the sky. Just look at it!"

Cloudhill was visible from the dining-room window;
the top was perfectly clear, there was not a cloud in
sight, and after some argument even the Colonel was
forced to agree that if the hill must be climbed this was

the right afternoon for the expedition. All the same, he was worried and when they had phoned up Craigrowan and prepared their picnic tea he followed them to the garage.

"Why not go somewhere else?" he suggested. "There are all sorts of good places for a picnic."

"But we've set our hearts upon Cloudhill," replied Hugo. He smiled and added, "There's something special about that hill. I want to go to the top."

"It will be all right, Daddy," said Patty soothingly.

"Oh well, don't be late," said the Colonel with a sigh. "You had better take my car—I won't be using it. Don't be late, will you?"

"Of course not," declared Hugo. "It won't take us long. You aren't really worried, are you, Uncle Thomas? I've done a lot of climbing—real climbing in the Alps —so I know a good deal about it. Surely you can trust me to take care of Patty."

"Oh, of course," agreed the Colonel hastily. "Of course you'll look after her—I know that—but don't be late."

Chapter 8

IT CERTAINLY was a beautiful afternoon; warm and still, with golden sunshine and an azure sky. Hugo and Patty went off together in the best of spirits; they parked the car at the bottom of the hill in a small disused quarry and got out. Patty picked up a stone and put it in the bag which was slung over her shoulder.

" What's that for? " asked Hugo.

" To put on the cairn," she replied. " It's the right thing to do when you climb a hill. You pick up a stone at the bottom and carry it to the top. Then you wish a wish. Everybody does it so the cairn grows higher— see? "

" If I take two stones can I have two wishes? "

" No, that's greedy," declared Patty, laughing.

Hugo laughed too. " I'll have a specially nice one then, and wish a specially nice wish. Look, Patty, this is a very special stone."

He showed her a curiously shaped red stone, with flecks of mica which glittered like diamonds in the brilliant sunshine, and Patty agreed that it would earn a specially nice wish.

At first their path followed the track of an old Roman road, overgrown with grass and brambles, but presently they left it and took a sheep track which wound upwards amongst heather and rocks. Little burns came trickling down and there were patches of sphagnum moss growing in the hollows. There was no actual climbing, for Cloudhill was rounded in contour, so they were able to chat quite comfortably as they went along.

" It's beautiful country," said Hugo. " I don't wonder you love it so much. I hope you won't find the country round Bellstead very tame. It has its own sort of beauty, but it isn't like this."

" We can come here for our holidays. We'll have to come often. You know that, don't you? "

" Whenever you want to," agreed Hugo.

After a while they sat down together on a bank beside a burn for there was no hurry (they had all the afternoon before them). Hugo took a letter out of his pocket; he had received it that morning from his mother. The letter was full of plans: plans for the wedding and for the alterations to Bellstead. There was so much to discuss that when Patty glanced at her watch she was surprised to discover it was after three.

" We must go on," she declared. " We said we wouldn't be late."

They rose and walked on.

The bank where they had been sitting was on the shoulder of the hill, sheltered by a ledge of rock and from here the summit was invisible, but presently they came to a ridge which led to the summit and turned to walk along it.

" Oh, look! " cried Patty, stopping and pointing.

Half an hour ago there had not been a cloud in the sky but now there was a thin gauzy cloud settled upon the top of the hill like a cap.

" How strange! " exclaimed Hugo. " It's quite eerie.

Where can it have come from? What causes it, I wonder."

Patty had heard various explanations of the phenomenon ranging from old MacLaggan's contention that it was a device of Auld Hornie to keep unwelcome visitors from trespassing upon his domain to that of her father's crony, Professor Brownlee, an expert in meteorology, whose theory was more scientific but much more difficult to understand.

" It's something to do with the shape of the hill," said Patty vaguely.

" Let's go and have a look at it."

" I don't think we ought to."

" Why not? It's fun. I want to see it nearer."

" But, Hugo——"

" We needn't go right into the mist if it seems too thick, but it isn't thick at all—just like a veil. You can see the rocks through it. Come on, Patty."

He strode on, hastening his steps, and Patty followed. They were still in brilliant sunshine, but after another fifty yards there were little ragged puffs of cloud all round them drifting this way and that in the still air.

" Hugo, stop! " cried Patty breathlessly. " Hugo, you don't understand! It may come down thicker any minute and we shall be lost! "

He looked round smiling. " Lost? How could we get lost on this funny little hill! Surely you aren't frightened? "

" No, but still——" said Patty dubiously.

He held out his hand and she took it. The hand was warm and comforting.

" Are you sure it's all right? " she asked. " I mean I

know you've done a lot of climbing—in Switzerland—
but this is different."

"I should just think it is!" said Hugo, laughing.
"This isn't climbing, it's an afternoon's walk, that's all.
Let's get to the top."

"We ought to go back."

"Why? What could happen to us?"

"There are boggy places," said Patty seriously.
"There are ledges of rock. One of us might fall
down——"

"Oh come on, Patty, be a sport!"

They went on, hand in hand, and at every step the
cloud became thicker; it was cold and damp and clammy.
Patty wished she had worn her tweed jacket but the
afternoon had been so warm that she had left it in the
car. She was wearing an open-necked shirt and a thin
woollen cardigan which was no protection at all. But
Hugo had said "Be a sport!" and this was a challenge
that Patty could not refuse. She had been brought up
with two boys and had prided herself on her ability to
keep up with them, to do all that they did and not be a
nuisance. Suddenly, however, Patty realised that this
adventure was very unwise indeed.

"Hugo, this is silly!" she exclaimed.

"Silly?"

"Yes, we can't see a thing. In fact, I think we've
come the wrong way. We're going in the wrong
direction."

"But we're still going up so we can't be wrong, can
we? Come on, Patty. It's fun."

It might be fun for Hugo with his warm tweed jacket
but for Patty it was no fun at all. Patty was cold and

frightened. " Hugo, please! " she exclaimed. " It really is dangerous! Let's go back."

" But we're almost at the top! "

For a few moments they stood still, undecided, and then a little whiff of air swept aside the cloud and they saw the hilltop crowned with its cairn of stones. It was quite near, scarcely a hundred yards from where they were standing, but between lay a small steep valley full of moss and boulders.

" There it is! " cried Hugo. " What did I tell you! It won't take five minutes———"

" It wouldn't if we were crows."

" What do you mean? "

" We're on the wrong ridge. Honestly, Hugo, it's farther than it looks and the valley is boggy. We'll have to go back."

" But we're almost there. I want to put my stone on the cairn and get my wish."

" We're not almost there. We can't cross the little valley . . . and the cloud is getting thicker. Please be sensible, Hugo."

" What on earth is the matter with you! " he exclaimed.

Patty was desperate. " I'm tired and cold and I want to go home."

" All right, you had better go back," agreed Hugo. " I'll nip across and put my stone on the cairn."

This was madness, of course. The only sane thing to do was to keep together. She began to explain but Hugo refused to listen.

" Off you go," said Hugo cheerfully. " You haven't got enough clothes on, that's the trouble, but if you keep moving you'll be all right. I shan't be long. I shall

probably catch you up before you're half-way down."
He released her hand—Patty was too proud to cling to
it—and strode off towards the cairn.

2

Patty watched Hugo for a few moments and then
turned back; it was the only thing to do. She kept to
the crest of the ridge, for here the cloud seemed thinner,
it came and went in drifts and eddies; but when she
turned to go down the hill she was immersed in a solid
bank of cloud. Patty was really frightened now, cold
and frightened, but it was no use standing still so she
went on slowly; then suddenly a stone turned under
her foot, she staggered and fell and rolled several yards.
She found herself clinging to a small rowan tree which
had its roots in a crevice. For a few moments she lay
there, gasping for breath and then she sat up.

Her ankle was painful—it was so extremely painful
that for a few moments she felt quite sick—but gradually
the pain wore off. It was a wrench not a sprain. Apart
from that Patty discovered that there was nothing the
matter with her—nothing at all. But the fall had shaken
her nerves for it had shown her what might have happened if she had not been extremely lucky. If she fell
again . . . if she really twisted her ankle badly . . . or
broke her leg . . .

Patty was tired and cold and frightened. Her teeth
began to chatter and the tears ran down her cheeks. She
got up and went on down the hill, feeling her way carefully, testing every step. After what seemed hours she
heard the tinkle of a little burn and, groping about,

found it running amongst the stones and the roots of heather. There was a sheep track beside the burn, so she followed it and got on faster. Presently she discovered that the cloud was becoming thinner, drifting raggedly in wafts of air, and a few moments later she emerged unexpectedly from its damp embrace.

Suddenly Patty was in clear air; there were blue skies above her and warm golden sunshine all round her. If she had not been so upset she might have been more interested in the phenomenon, but as it was she was just unutterably thankful. She went on a bit farther and then sat down on a rock—her knees felt weak and she was trembling all over.

"You donkey!" said Patty to herself. "You idiot! What are you making such a fuss about? You're all right now. It was beastly while it lasted but it's all over and you're perfectly safe. For goodness' sake pull up your socks and be a man!"

Thus adjured Patty pulled up her socks. She wiped her eyes. She opened her bag and taking out a little comb ran it through her damp and tousled curls. She found her powder-compact and powdered her nose. A touch of lipstick completed her toilet. Oddly enough these small attentions to her personal appearance helped Patty to " be a man." The sunshine helped too, it was warm and comforting. In fact, it was so warm that the rock upon which she was sitting was hot to the touch. This gave her an idea, and taking off her cardigan she spread it out to dry; steam rose from it gently in the still air.

A rabbit came out of its hole and began to nibble the grass; it did not seem the least afraid of Patty. The rabbit completed the cure—it was company. Patty watched it with pleasure for it was quite a long time since she had seen a rabbit. Probably, because of its isolated abode, this particular rabbit had escaped the disease which had wiped out its relations and was breeding a family upon Cloudhill. Patty was a farmer's daughter, so she was aware that rabbits were "pests" but she could not help feeling that there was something rather nice about rabbits.

3

By this time Patty had recovered sufficiently to take her bearings and to realise that she was only a few minutes' walk from the little quarry where they had left the car. She went on down the hill and found it without any difficulty. There it stood, dear shabby old car! The rug, the picnic basket and Patty's jacket were all inside . . . and the door was not locked. Hugo ought to have locked the doors but he had not done so. Patty spread the rug, took out the basket and sat down to have her tea.

So far she had not given a thought to her companion, but now she began to feel angry. How foolish he had been! How stubborn and inconsiderate! She was used to taking her chance with boys and sharing in their adventurous pursuits, but even when they were quite young Rae and Will had felt responsible for her; neither of them would have dreamt of deserting her, or leaving her alone, cold and frightened, in the mist. They might have grumbled and called her " a little idiot," but they would have stuck to her and brought her safely down.

Yes, she was angry with Hugo—very angry indeed.

Patty ate two honey sandwiches; she drank a cup of tea and felt a great deal better. There was still no sign of Hugo, and presently her vexation gave place to anxiety—what could have happened to him? If all had gone well he should have been here long ago. In fact he should have been here before her for she had wasted quite a time wandering in the mist. What if he were lost? What if he had sprained his ankle—as she had so nearly done? What if he had fallen into a bog and was lying there helpless?

Patty could see the top of the hill from where she was sitting and she noted that the cloud was thickening and spreading. Other clouds, dark and angry, were coming up from behind Craigrowan Forest and rolling across the sky.

Daddy will be worried to death, thought Patty miserably.

What was the best thing to do—that was the question. It was useless to go back and look for Hugo; she had no idea where to look. Should she go to the nearest farm for help or should she go home? How long should she wait before she took action? If she waited too long it would be dark. Patty walked up and down restlessly, glancing at her watch every few minutes. The hands seemed to move very slowly.

I shall go home, thought Patty at last. I shall wait ten minutes more and then go home. Why should Daddy be worried into fits because Hugo is such an idiot?

It was at this very moment that Patty heard a cheerful hail and the cause of all the trouble appeared. He was coming along the road, striding out with his unusually long legs and twirling his stick.

89

"Hallo!" cried Hugo. "Here I am! You weren't worrying, were you? I came down the other side of the hill so I had to leg it back. I suppose you've had tea?"

"Yes," said Patty.

"Good. I hoped you wouldn't wait for me. Nothing like a cup of tea when you're tired and cold. You hadn't enough clothes on; that was the trouble."

He smiled at her, but she did not return the smile.

"I say, you aren't cross, are you?" he asked in sudden anxiety.

"No," said Patty untruthfully.

"Good," said Hugo. "I thought you seemed a little put out . . . but you understood, didn't you? I mean we were so near the top that it seemed a pity to go back without making it."

"Did you make it?"

"Well, of course! No difficulty at all. I put my stone on the top of the cairn and wished a wish. That was the right thing, wasn't it? It was fun; you should have been with me, Patty. Another time you must wear a tweed jacket—that's the proper kit for the hills."

There won't be another time, thought Patty. Aloud she said, "We must go home at once. Daddy will be frightfully worried."

"Worried? Why should he worry? I mean, he'll know you're perfectly safe with me. If you'd been alone it would have been different."

Patty was silent.

"You had no difficulty in finding your way down, did you?" asked Hugo.

Patty was getting into the car; she did not reply.

All this time Patty's rage had been growing and it

was only by a superhuman effort that she managed to control her tongue. If Hugo had returned muddy and bedraggled with his tail between his legs she would have forgiven him freely, but he had returned with the air of a conqueror. Hugo had proved himself right; there had been no difficulty in getting to the top and he had come down safely. He had added to his sins by telling her that she was not properly clad for an expedition of this nature. (Patty had realised this herself, but to be told so by Hugo was different.) Last but not least, he had sealed his doom by saying that she would be perfectly safe with him. Perfectly safe!

He got into the car beside her and started the engine.

" We had better go straight home, I suppose," said Hugo. " I mean there wouldn't be time to stop at a pub? "

" No, there wouldn't."

" Uncle Thomas *does* worry a bit, doesn't he? "

" Yes."

There was silence for a few moments while Hugo manœuvred the car on to the road. Then he continued in a more doubtful tone, " So perhaps it might be just as well not to tell him that I went to the top and you didn't. He might think—I mean it might be better not to—to mention it? "

" Much better."

" Mum's the word, then," said Hugo cheerfully.

Patty said nothing.

" Mum's the word," repeated Hugo with a slight show of anxiety.

" I won't tell anybody," said Patty.

PART TWO

The Wild Goose Chase

Chapter 9

WILL'S DECISION to go for a walking tour in France was not the result of a sudden whim, nor was it entirely aimless. Ever since that day in the old play-room—when Patty had given him Rae's letter to read—the mystery had been at the back of his mind. Sometimes he had almost forgotten about it, and then quite suddenly he had remembered. Will had convinced Patty that the letter was unimportant—merely a scrawl dashed off by a man in a hurry who was excited at the prospect of leave—but in so doing he had fallen a prey to the infection. Will had known Rae so well—and Rae was no fool! He was bold and impulsive but it was not like him to talk wildly—far less to write wildly! You might think him a mad-cap but afterwards you usually discovered that there was method in his madness . . . perhaps Rae had written that letter with a purpose. Perhaps he had intended to prepare the way for a disclosure of importance and wanted Patty's support.

Thinking it over and considering the matter, Will decided that he would go to France and see the farmer with whom Rae had been billeted. The man might know nothing, but at any rate it would be a relief to see him and talk to him about Rae. It was a long time ago but Leyrisse was sure to remember Rae, for Rae was not the sort of person who was easily forgotten.

No harm could come of it, thought Will, for he would tell nobody of his intention; if he found out something he could either disclose it or keep it under his hat; if he found out nothing nobody would be a penny the worse. Will might have hesitated to probe into another man's past, but he could not imagine Rae doing anything he could be ashamed of. Besides, the letter had said quite definitely that the writer was looking forward to telling his family the secret. Will could not remember the exact words of the letter but that was implied.

There was no need to tell the Elliot Murrays that he was going away, for since Hugo's arrival the pleasant habit of "dropping in " at Langford had been abandoned —and apparently they had not missed him at all! (They had Hugo, of course, thought Will bitterly.) The only person to be informed and consulted was his father, and Mr. Hastie was in favour of the plan.

At the last moment, just before leaving Broadmeadows, Will had a sudden impulse to speak to Patty (it seemed odd to go off like this without telling Patty he was going), so he rang up Langford. The telephone was answered by Colonel Elliot Murray himself.

" Patty is out," said the Colonel. " She and Hugo have gone up Cloudhill this afternoon. They're having a picnic. If you ring again about six you'll get her."

" Lovely day for Cloudhill," declared Will with forced cheerfulness.

" Well, I don't know," said the Colonel doubtfully. " It looked all right at lunch-time but there's a cloud on the top now."

" Don't worry, sir," said Will. " Patty knows Cloudhill. They won't go up if there's a cloud on the top, they'll have their picnic somewhere else."

" Yes," agreed the Colonel a trifle more cheerfully. " Yes, that's true. Patty knows the ropes . . . you'll ring up later? "

" I can't," explained Will. " I'm just off for a holiday. There's no message except to tell Patty and to give her my love."

Will had expected Colonel Elliot Murray to show some interest in his trip, but very little interest was shown. The fact was the Colonel's thoughts were elsewhere. " I'll tell her," he said vaguely. " Have a good time, Will. We'll see you when you get home."

" Don't worry, sir," repeated Will. " Patty wouldn't go up if there was a cloud——"

" I know. I'm not worrying at all," declared Patty's father untruthfully.

2

Will had not expected to enjoy his holiday, the expedition to France had not been undertaken for enjoyment—but the skies were blue and the sun was warm and there was a pleasant breeze. As he strode along the road from Calais his spirits rose and his troubles seemed lighter.

It was good to be free; he was as free as a bird. There was no need to stick to the main road, there was no need to eat at stated hours. He could go as he pleased. Lately Will had been wishing—in a vague sort of way—that he had not left the Service. He was fond of his home and very fond indeed of his father, but he missed the companionship of men of his own age and the varied interests of Army life. Now, as he strode along with his haversack on his back, he realised that these thoughts had been foolish. One must look forward, not backward, and above all one must not indulge in self-pity nor allow oneself to get in a groove.

This was new country to Will. He had travelled in many lands but never in France—except to rush through in a train—so he was interested in all he saw and found a peculiar beauty in the long straight roads bordered with poplars. The flatness of the country was a change from his own wild moory hills. He enjoyed stopping at little inns for a meal or a drink and if the inn attracted him he could stay there for the night. Once or twice he walked all night and rested during the day.

Will's war had been fought in Africa and Italy so he had never been closely in touch with the people of this part of the world—they seemed more strange than the country itself—but most of them were eager to be friendly. Some of them offered him lifts and chatted as they went along. One old farmer who was returning from market with a pig in the back of his ancient and dilapidated van offered Will a bed for the night and Will, who was ready for any sort of unusual adventure, accepted the offer and slumbered peacefully in an enormous feather-bed.

Long ago Will had shared a French governess with Rae and Patty, so he had learnt to speak French fairly well and with a reasonably good accent (Rae and Patty had learnt far more, of course, for she had stayed at Langford and they had been with her all the time). Since then Will had had no occasion to speak French and had been under the impression that he had for-gotten every word—but now it was gradually coming back to mind. He discovered that he could ask for what he wanted and could understand what was said to him if it was said slowly and distinctly. The rapid flow of words when they spoke to each other defeated him entirely. All this was rather amusing—or at least Will found it so. He was thoroughly enjoying his holiday and he was enjoying the food with its strange flavours, so different from the "good plain cooking" which was served at his father's table by good plain Mrs. McTaggie, the housekeeper at Broadmeadows.

In this pleasant and casual manner Will sauntered along and gradually approached the village of Badlieu where he hoped to find Jean Leyrisse. He approached it eventually in a large car which picked him up on the road. The car belonged to Mr. and Mrs. Morgan Tessell, of New Haven, Connecticut, who were doing a tour of Europe. Like most Americans, they were friendly and kind and enormously interested in their fellow creatures. They were interested in Will and questioned him in an uninhibited manner about his adventures and his future plans. They were even more interested when Will told them. Oddly enough, these complete strangers were the first people to hear about the "wild-goose chase" . . . but perhaps it was not so very odd after all for it is often possible to talk to strangers about confidential matters which one would not mention to one's nearest and dearest and as it was nearly a week since he had con-versed with anybody in his own language he was feeling pent-up inside.

The Tessells were sympathetic and encouraging.

They, too, were on a "wild-goose chase" for they were on their way to Metz, where they hoped to discover some distant cousins. Already they had discovered a distant cousin in the wilds of Wales and had found him a delightful relative.

"Morgan's technique is to talk to everybody," declared Mrs. Tessell. "He keeps on asking questions."

"They don't mind," explained Mr. Tessell. "We were told before we left home that Britishers were like clams—but it just isn't true, or at least they're much easier to open than any clam I ever saw. French people are a little more difficult—maybe it's the language—but you can open them up too if you take a little trouble. For instance, there was that lady we met up with last evening at the hotel; Madame Fournier was her name. Well, I got a whole lot of information out of her. I don't say it was all to the point, but it was very, very interesting. One thing she told me—and it may be useful to you, Mr. Hastie—she told me about Badlieu. There's a very ancient church there; it dates way back to the Normans, Madame Fournier said."

"I don't see how that's going to be useful to Mr. Hastie," put in Mrs. Tessell. "It's that farmer he wants to see."

"The priest might be useful, Ireen. He's called Father Anton; he lives next door to the church and shows people around. It might be a good plan for Mr. Hastie to talk to the priest and ask him a few simple questions. No harm ever comes of asking questions," added Mr. Tessell with conviction.

"Harm comes when you start giving advice," said Mrs. Tessel, laughing.

Mr. Tessell laughed too, though not quite so heartily.

Obviously this was a joke, and on inquiring into the matter Will was informed that Madame Fournier's daughter had a squint and Mr. Tessell had advised her to take the child to an oculist and to have the unfortunate tendency corrected without delay.

"She felt badly about it," admitted Mr. Tessell. "But I would have felt badly if I hadn't told her."

Will saw the point. He thought it an interesting side-light upon human nature.

It had been arranged that Will was to be dropped some miles from Badlieu to complete his journey on foot, but by this time the Tessells were so friendly that they insisted on going out of their way to take Will to his destination. So Will was dropped at the priest's house, and after many expressions of good-will on both sides his new friends drove away. It seemed sad to think that in the ordinary course of events he would never see them again.

Chapter 10

FATHER ANTON was sitting in his study, writing, when Will was shown in. He was a very old man, his face was wrinkled like a wizened apple but his light blue eyes were bright. The small room was in confusion, there were books and papers upon every chair, so that Father Anton, after asking his unexpected visitor to be seated, was obliged to clear a chair for him to sit upon. This he did by tipping its contents on to the floor. Its contents, Will noticed, was a very large hat-box full of moss—which seemed a strange object to find in the little priest's study.

"Ça ne fait rien," declared Father Anton, viewing the resultant mess with equanimity, and he added, still speaking in his own language, " My sister will sweep it up. Sit down, my friend. Be at ease and tell me how I can help you."

Will had hoped that Father Anton might be able to speak English but in this he was disappointed.

" I am sorry," said the priest, shaking his head sadly. " Often I have wished I could speak your language. There were English soldiers in the village during the war but I could not learn to speak to them—not a word! It was too difficult, you see. They spoke so quickly and the pronounciation was so strange."

He paused and looked at Will doubtfully. "But you cannot understand what I say?"

"Je comprends assez bien—si vous parlez—lente-ment," declared Will, waving his hands wildly. "Je ne peux pas—parler—moi-même."

"But you speak well! Your accent is excellent! I can see that all you require is practice. What can I do for you, my friend?"

"Rae Elliot Murray," said Will slowly. "Perhaps you knew him. He was here. He lived at the farm of Jean Leyrisse."

The old man nodded. "Oui, c'est ça. I knew him well. He was a fine young man; one would not forget him in a hurry."

"He was my friend. I would like——"

"Ah yes! You would like to visit his grave. But that is easy. I will show you."

Will was surprised; he had presumed Rae's grave to be in one of the large military cemeteries where so many of his companions lay (all he had hoped to get from Father Anton was information). He tried to explain and at last he managed to make his meaning plain.

"But yes, I can tell you," nodded the priest. "I can tell you many things about the young man—his name is very difficult for me to say. He was a fine young man, light-hearted and full of the joy of life. War is a sad business."

"You said you would show me his grave."

"Yes, he lies here, in our little churchyard. Jean Leyrisse arranged it with the authorities—how, I do not know. I hope there is no trouble about it?"

Will shook his head.

"Ah, good! For my part I liked the idea. It seemed natural at the time. Come, my friend, and I will show you." The old man seized his battered hat and made for the door.

"Vos souliers!" exclaimed Will.

"Ah yes," agreed Father Anton, looking down at his feet and smiling. "How fortunate that you noticed! My sister would have been annoyed if I had gone out in my slippers; she made them for me herself, you see. She is a good kind creature, but she is annoyed with me when I am absent-minded—and alas I am often absent-minded—but there are so many things to think about and when one becomes old one cannot think of many things all at once."

2

The priest had been changing his shoes as he spoke and now he stood up and announced himself ready. "It is not far," he declared. "He lies in a sheltered corner of our little churchyard and Jean Leyrisse lies beside him. To me that seems good: the old French farmer and the young English soldier—n'est-ce pas? But come, my friend, we are wasting time." He shouted to an unseen presence in the back premises that he was going out, and led the way across his garden.

"Jean Leyrisse is dead?" asked Will, hoping he had misunderstood, for the whole object of his coming had been to speak to the old farmer.

"Alas, yes! Jean Leyrisse is dead. It was an acute inflammation of the lungs. He died only a few weeks after your friend was killed. That was the reason they sold the farm and departed, What else could they do, poor things? It was impossible for Julie and her mother to manage the farm themselves—one could see that—but what a loss to my parish! Ah, what a loss! They were good to my poor people, you see. It was a loss to me also for they were kind to me. Every week I went to dinner; it was a definite arrangement—every Wednesday. Madame Leyrisse was an excellent cook." He shook his head sadly. Obviously he had enjoyed his weekly dinner at the Leyrisses' farm.

" Madame Leyrisse is dead too? "

" No, no! She has gone away—she and her daughter—but no doubt you know this already. How my sister would scold me for chattering! She is always telling me I talk too much."

It was true that he was a talker. He had said Will required practice in speaking French but it was obvious that he would not get much practice while he was in the old priest's company. All the same it was beginning to come back to him—words and phrases that he thought he had forgotten sprang into his mind—and although he was aware that what he said was " all wrong " grammatically he had ceased to care.

" There is the church," continued the priest. " It is old and very beautiful as you can see. Later I will show you the church, but first I will show you the grave of your friend. It is this way. How glad I am that you came to-day for you will see the flowers! Yesterday was his birthday—as you probably know—so the flowers will still be fresh. They do not last long in the warm sunshine. It seems a pity——"

" Flowers? " asked Will when he could get a word in edgeways.

" Roses. Yes, it is always red roses—and she never forgets. Usually she brings them herself, but if it is impossible for her to come she sends them to me in a large box carefully packed in moss. She relies upon me to put them upon his grave if she cannot come herself."

" Who sends them? " asked Will, but Father Anton was not listening. Perhaps he was a little deaf.

" It is a long journey," he explained. " She cannot come and go in a day so she must stay the night at the auberge in the village and this costs money. They are not very well off. Sometimes there are other things to prevent her from coming; her mother is not strong."

So far it had not been as difficult as Will had expected, for his guide had done all the talking (and luckily he spoke so clearly and distinctly that he was easy to understand), but now there were all sorts of questions Will wanted to ask. He was struggling to find words when his guide stopped at a grave in a corner of the little churchyard. Upon it lay a large wreath of beautiful red roses. The cross which marked it was of white marble and bore Rae's name but nothing more.

" We did not know," explained Father Anton. " None of us knew what else to put, nor how to spell the name of his regiment. It seemed better to put nothing than to put it wrong. But you can tell me, n'est-ce pas? You can write it on a paper, very clearly, and I will have it done. I will see to it myself so that there will be no mistake. How glad I am that you have come! It has worried me considerably that only his name and nothing more——"

" Padre," said Will, trying to stem the tide. " Ecoutez un moment, je vous prie."

" Yes, yes, what is it? "

" Is it permitted that I address you as Padre? "

" Why not, my friend? That is what the English soldiers called me—and you are English. Perhaps you too are a soldier? You have the bearing of one who has———"

" Padre, listen! Who sent the roses? "

" But I have told you! It is she, the widow of your friend; she sends them every year on his birthday—or brings them herself if it is possible."

" His widow! " exclaimed Will in stupefied tones.

" But of course. Who else? "

" Rae's widow! But Rae was not married! "

" He was married," declared Father Anton.

" There is some mistake! "

" There is no mistake. I can tell you that—none better —for it was I who married them. Only a handful of people were present at the ceremony: Julie's parents and her brother—who was afterwards killed in the Résistance—and Monsieur le Colonel and one or two other officers. The marriage was very quiet—that goes without saying—for were we not in the midst of war? It was no occasion for feasting and gaiety. One was not in the mood for such things. But in spite of the quietness —or perhaps because of it—the marriage was very beautiful. The bride was beautiful and the bridegroom was handsome—and both were so young."

Will had been trying to interrupt this monologue and now, when the priest paused for breath, he tried again, but it was useless. Before Will could find words the priest continued:

"Both were so young," he repeated sadly. "There was a radiance in their faces like a light shining from within. It seemed to me that those two were made for each other; it seemed to me that le bon Dieu intended the marriage to take place. You see, monsieur, it was not as if they were strangers to me. I had known Julie since she was a little child, so I knew she could be trusted, and my instinct told me that this man she had chosen was good all through. So when they came to me and said they wanted to be married I consented. What else could I do?"

"It was legal?"

"Legal!" cried Father Anton indignantly. "But of course! What do you think? It was wartime and all the country was in a mess, but even in wartime one must keep the law. You may see the record if you doubt my word."

"Forgive me, Padre," said Will. "I do not doubt your word. It is because I am so—so (what on earth was surprised? Oh yes.) Parce que je suis étonné," declared Will emphatically.

"But why? Why should you be astonished? Is it not natural for young people to marry? It is true that it happened very quickly, but in those days everything happened quickly. There was so little time and none of us knew how long we had to live."

Will nodded.

"There was a feeling of urgency," added Father Anton.

"Yes," agreed Will. He knew, only too well, that

feeling of urgency, the feeling that if anything was to be done it must be done at once—or it might never be done at all.

For a few moments they were silent. Then Will said, " I must see her."

" You must see her? "

" Yes," nodded Will.

" Whom must you see? "

" The wife of my friend, of course."

" But that is impossible! I have told you she is not here any longer. She has gone away."

" All the same I must see her," declared Will. " You will tell me where she lives and I will——"

" I cannot tell you that."

" You must tell me! " cried Will. " We cannot—just —leave it. I must see her—and—and talk to her. Don't you understand, Padre? "

" Mais oui, mon ami, I understand very well that you want to see Julie, but I cannot help you."

" You can tell me her address."

The old man shook his head. " No, I do not know her address. I would tell you if I could, for it would be good and right for you to talk to Julie—but I cannot help you."

Will stared at him incredulously. " You mean you have forgotten her address? "

" I never knew it. Julie never told me."

" But, Padre—— "

" I can see that this seems strange to you, but none the less it is true. When Madame Leyrisse left here she bought a villa in the south and that is where they live— she and Julie. I know no more."

"A villa in the south!" exclaimed Will. "That is all you know?"

"It is strange," agreed Father Anton, gazing at Will in a bewildered manner. "Now that I think about it I can see that it is very strange indeed. I can see that I ought to know their address—but it never occurred to me to ask."

"You lost touch with them——"

"But no, I have never lost touch with them! Once a year Julie comes with her roses; she tells me about her mother and we walk round the garden together—we talk of old times before the war. Then Julie goes away. A year passes—years pass quickly when one is old—and then she comes again." He sighed and added, "Sometimes she does not come."

"Has she never once mentioned the town where she lives? One would think she would have—have mentioned its name——"

"One would think so. Yes, indeed, it would have been only natural. I can see that now." He hesitated and then added, "One begins to think that Julie withheld the information deliberately . . . and yet there seems no reason for it."

Will had the same idea. She had withheld her address deliberately. It would be easy enough, of course. Now that he had seen Father Anton he realised how easy it would be. Father Anton never asked questions; he was absolutely devoid of curiosity. He liked to talk, not to listen, and a word here and there kept him talking happily for hours.

"There seems no reason for it," repeated the priest : bewildered tones.

There could be only one reason—or so Will thought—Madame Leyrisse and her daughter did not want to be found . . . but somehow or other he must find them.

"What am I to do!" he exclaimed in despair.

"I am sorry, my friend. It grieves me that I cannot help you—but there it is. Julie comes and goes like the swallows, and like the swallows she is a welcome visitor. It is delightful to see her and I look forward eagerly to her arrival. Yesterday when the box came by post I felt sad. Yes, I felt sad for I knew she would not come herself. It will be a year before I can hope to see the dear child—and I am getting no younger. Who knows if I shall still be here!"

"The box!" cried Will. "Is there not an address on the box?"

"It is possible——" began Father Anton doubtfully.

Will did not wait to hear more. He left the priest standing in the churchyard and ran back to the house—and it was as well that he had hurried for he found the priest's sister on her knees in the study sweeping up the moss. Already the paper in which the box had been wrapped was crumpled and torn and pressed into the waste-paper basket ready for burning.

"What are you doing?" exclaimed the old woman angrily. "Is there not enough mess already without you strewing paper all over the floor! Who are you, may I ask? What right have you to be here? Where have you come from? Leave that box alone. It is quite a good box and when I have dried it carefully . . ."

Will did not listen. He was examining the box; he was smoothing out the crumpled paper. There was no name upon it, no address, the only clue was the postmark, and even that had been partly obliterated by the dampness of the moss . . . but it was the only clue, and although Will could make nothing of it himself he had hopes that the post office authorities might help him. He remembered reading somewhere—probably in a detective story—that post office authorities were able to trace postmarks with very little data to come and go on, so he removed the label very carefully and put it in his pocket.

By this time Father Anton had arrived and was arguing with his sister; or at least she was arguing and he was endeavouring to defend himself. The conversation, carried on rapidly and fiercely, was unintelligible to Will but their demeanour was easily understood. Will disliked " scenes "; he was a man of peace; so he took his leave hastily and walked down to the village where he found a very comfortable little auberge in which to spend the night.

Chapter 11

THE NEXT morning Will woke early and after his coffee
and rolls (which to tell the truth seemed a poor substitute
for his usual Scottish breakfast of porridge and bacon
and eggs) he hurried off to the post office to see if the
postmark on the label could be identified. Although it
was still early they were busy, but he managed to get
hold of a young clerk who was interested in the unusual
request.

" Is it a police matter? " he asked, his bright brown
eyes gleaming intelligently through his spectacles.

" No, just some friends I want to find. I have been
away for years and they have moved," explained Will.
He had thought out this explanation beforehand; it
seemed a bit thin but it was the best he could do. If the
post office authorities could not help him he might have
to go to the police, but that would be the last resort.

" I will try," said the young clerk, looking at the label
doubtfully. " If monsieur will leave it with me I will do
my best. There is not a great deal of the postmark to
be seen."

Will agreed that there was very little. He was turning
away feeling somewhat hopeless when it suddenly
occurred to him to inquire if there happened to be a letter
for him. He had given his father *Poste Restante, Badlieu,*

as his first address—and although it was unlikely that his father had written to him so soon after his departure it seemed foolish not to ask. Much to his surprise a letter was produced and handed across the counter. The letter was addressed in his father's writing and was extremely bulky. This also was surprising, and slightly alarming, for although Mr. Hastie was a good correspondent and had always written regularly to Will when he was serving overseas it seemed strange that he could have found much to say so soon after Will's departure from Broadmeadows.

Crossing the street to a little café, Will sat down upon a bench beneath a lime tree and opened the letter forthwith.

Broadmeadows,
Torfoot

Dear Will,

No doubt you will be surprised to receive such a long epistle from me, especially as we agreed before you left home that except for an occasional postcard there would be no need to correspond while you were away. The fact is I am exceedingly dull without you, my dear fellow, and having news of an interesting nature to impart I could not forbear to write. The news concerns our friends at Langford—let me hasten to assure you that they are all in good health.

(Will paused here to chuckle, for obviously the news—whatever it was—had pleased the old boy considerably. Only when Mr. Hastie was in particularly good form were his letters couched in this Pickwickian style.

Anyhow there was no need for Will to be alarmed, so he ordered a cup of coffee and continued to read the letter at his ease.)

This morning, whilst still at breakfast, I was informed by our good Mistress McTaggie that Miss Elliot Murray had called to see me. Naturally I was surprised—nay, apprehensive—and hastened to the front door where Mistress McTaggie had left her. (By the way I really must " speak " to Mistress McTaggie, albeit tactfully, about this inhospitable manner of treating visitors.)

It seemed to me that Patty was disturbed, but she accepted my invitation to come in and share my frugal meal saying she had not partaken of breakfast before leaving home as she was so very anxious to see me—and soon we were sitting together at table as cozy as you please. " There's nothing wrong, I hope? " I asked (though as a matter of fact my fears on this score had been allayed by the sight of my unexpected, though always welcome, guest tucking into her porridge very heartily). "Not wrong, exactly," she replied. " I mean nobody is ill or anything. I just want you to help me." I assured her that I was hers to command. " It's rather difficult," declared Patty. " But you're a lawyer, aren't you, so you'll know how to do it properly. I've done all I can, but he doesn't understand. He says girls always shilly and shally, but I don't. I mean I may have shillied but I don't intend to shally. I thought perhaps you could explain."

" Perhaps I could if I knew what to explain," I

replied with caution. "Oh, I thought I had told you," said Patty. "I'm a bit upset this morning. Daddy won't like it, you see, and I hate doing anything to hurt Daddy. Of course if I told Daddy the whole story he would understand, but I can't do that. I can't tell you either because I promised Hugo I wouldn't tell anybody."

By this time light had begun to dawn upon your thick-headed parent. "You've decided not to marry Hugo?" I suggested. Patty nodded. "I can't," she declared. "I can't and I won't—and that's flat." It could not have been flatter. "And you want me to explain this to Hugo?" "Yes," said Patty. "I've told him. I told him last night after the parents had gone to bed but he wouldn't believe I was serious. It's because he thinks he's marvellous, that's why. Everybody thinks he's marvellous. Daddy thinks he's marvellous. I thought he was marvellous too—until yesterday afternoon. I expect you think he's marvellous." I assured Patty that it had never occurred to me that there was anything marvellous about the young man and that I welcomed her decision not to marry him. "Really?" cried Patty, opening her eyes very wide—her eyes are a particularly delightful colour as I dare say you may have noticed—"You mean you don't think I'm silly?" I replied that, on the contrary, I thought she was wise. "Oh, what a comfort!" she exclaimed. "Then you're on my side, aren't you? That makes it ever so much easier."

We discussed the matter further. I confess I should have liked to know what occurred yesterday afternoon to upset the idol from his pedestal but Patty is a young woman of integrity and, having given her word, refused to divulge the secret. "I just want you to tell him, that's all," said Patty firmly. "I know it's asking a lot but you could do it better than anybody." Obviously this was flattery, and flattery to gain her ends, which was very reprehensible, but your soft-hearted parent fell for it all the same. "Oh good!" exclaimed Patty. "You *are* a darling—and if you could possibly tell the parents as well I'd be terribly grateful."

This was a bit more than I had bargained for, and I might have hesitated to undertake the task of breaking the unwelcome tidings to "the parents" had not two large crystalline tears escaped from my visitor's eyes and rolled down her cheeks. I was lost, of course, absolutely lost. I was all the more lost because she mopped them up hastily and apologised for "being silly."

Well, that is my news and I hope you are as pleased as I am. I know you agree that the young man is not nearly good enough for Patty—even with Langford in his pocket. The detailed story of how I accomplished my mission must await your return. Suffice to say the young man showed himself in somewhat disagreeable colours, which confirmed my opinion of his character.

My interview with the Colonel was most distressing. I can't write about it, Will—or at least not in this facetious vein. I see now what a fool I was not to have understood why the Colonel was so set on this marriage. All the same Patty is well out of it, there is no doubt of that.

This letter has overflowed the bounds. It is after

midnight and high time for your aged parent to be in bed.

All my love, dearest boy,

William Reid Hastie

PS.: I have not said I hope you are enjoying your travels (without a donkey) but that goes without saying. W.R.H.

There was so much food for thought in this letter that Will sat on the bench beneath the lime tree for a long time and allowed his coffee to become stone cold.

Chapter 12

THE DAY was warm and the sun was very bright; the street sloped upwards with shops on either side—gaily painted shops with glittering windows. There were flower shops and grocers' shops, there was a small but very elegant establishment with one gay nonsense of a hat displayed in the window. There was a shop with all manner of fancy goods and cheap toys, Pour les Cadeaux. There were cakes and sweets in the window of the pâtisserie. There were little restaurants with striped awnings and tables and chairs which overflowed on to the pavement and obstructed the passage of pedestrians.

This was Nivennes—a small market-town in the South of France—and it was here that Will hoped to find Rae's wife.

Will had arrived here by train the night before and had booked himself a room at the old-fashioned hotel near the station. It had started life as a coaching inn and had seen its best days, but they had given him a good meal and a large room on the first floor overlooking the yard. He had been tired last night after the long journey but now he was rested and refreshed and ready to resume his search.

Remembering the advice of Mr. Morgan Tessell, Will had already begun to ask questions. He had asked the manager of the hotel if by any chance he knew Madame Leyrisse. Monsieur Bénoit shook his head sadly. He knew many ladies in Nivennes—and enumerated them upon his fat fingers for Will's benefit —but he did not know Madame Leyrisse. But stay! cried Monsieur Bénoit, struck by a sudden brilliant idea. There was the English lady who lived in an apartment in Rue St. Simon! She was called "Mees Vairnon." Obviously she must be the one! Will repeated patiently that he was looking for Madame Leyrisse—and escaped from the garrulous little hôtelier as quickly as he could.

That was last night. This morning Will had repeated his question to the waiter and the chambermaid. The waiter who had brought Will his meagre breakfast was a surly individual and could not—or would not—understand what Will meant. The chambermaid was much more pleasant but alas she had never heard of Madame Leyrisse! Then she exclaimed in triumph. But of course! Why had she not thought of this before? There was the book of the telephone, was there not? Would Monsieur like her to fetch the book from the little kiosk in the hall and look for the name?

Monsieur's eyes brightened. He thoroughly approved of the idea. So the book was fetched and they searched for the name together, but there was no Leyrisse in it— no, not one.

All this was somewhat discouraging. Will began to wonder whether Madame Leyrisse and her daughter lived in Nivennes. The postmark on the label had been identified but that was not to say that the person who had posted it was a resident in the little town. She might have been here on a visit, or she might have come here on purpose to post the parcel so that the post-mark would give no clue to her whereabouts . . . but Will could not believe that. It was too far-fetched. Even if the idea had crossed her mind (which was unlikely) it certainly would never occur to her that Father Anton would notice the postmark. He was not that sort of man.

The glare in the street was terrific to Will's unac-customed eyes so he went into a small café and sat down near the window. He would have liked a glass of water, for there is nothing so good as water when one is thirsty, but he was ashamed to ask for water so he ordered wine. The wine was cold and golden and tasted of muscat grapes. It was delicious. He asked in his laborious French if it was grown in the neighbourhood.

" Mais oui," said the waiter, nodding, and he added that the wine was a speciality of Nivennes. The vineyard was on the hill behind the town. It was a very famous vineyard and belonged to a family named Delormes— had belonged to them for generations. Did Monsieur like the wine? Would he have another glass?

Monsieur liked it immensely; he would have another glass.

2

The street, which had been fairly quiet when Will set out from the hotel, was now filling up rapidly with cars and bicyles and heavy lorries piled with crates of fruit and vegetables. The pavements were crowded with people of all sorts and conditions. It was amusing to

watch them, thought Will. Occasionally a passer-by
would recognise a friend in the throng and the two
would pause and greet one another with cries of delight
and astonishment—which would not have been out of
place had they been blood-brothers, parted for years,
and meeting unexpectedly in the jungle.

Will was enjoying himself now; he found it very
amusing. He would have enjoyed himself even more if
this had been an ordinary holiday visit to the little town
. . . if he had not felt obliged to ask questions.

Bother that woman, thought Will. I've got her on
my brain. She's become an obsession.

Up to now his one idea had been to find Rae's wife—
he could not think of her as Rae's widow—but now he
began to wonder what would happen if he found her?
Would the Elliot Murrays be pleased or would it just
upset them and cause a lot of trouble? It's nearly twelve
years, thought Will. Quite possibly she may have
married someone else. He sat and thought, gazing out
at the bright glare of the street and the people passing
to and fro till he was almost dizzy.

What would she be like? He considered that carefully
because it was important—but how could he tell what
she was like until he had seen her—and by then it
would be too late. Here and now (Will realised) he
must make up his mind quite definitely whether to
advance or retreat for he had almost reached the point of
no return—almost but not quite. He could go back to
the hotel, pack his haversack and walk out of Nivennes
without another word and nobody would ever know he
had been there. It would be quite easy—and perhaps it
would be better for everybody. Shall I—or shall I not?

thought Will. The daughter of a French farmer! Would the mere fact of her existence be any comfort to the Elliot Murrays—or the reverse. She might be quite impossible—but no, that was a foolish thought because she was Rae's wife. Rae was fastidious—more so than anybody Will had ever known—so she must be all right.

What about Rae? thought Will. Would Rae want me to find her and dig her out and take her home to Langford?

At first Will could not answer this question, but it was a habit of his to turn things round and look at them from the other person's point of view. Let's turn it back to front, thought Will. Supposing this was Rae, sitting here in this café at this table; supposing I had been killed. Would I want Rae to find my wife and take her home to Broadmeadows? Put like this, back to front, he saw the answer quite clearly.

3

The waiter was hovering near the open doorway and came at Will's signal. Monsieur would like another glass of wine?

" Non," said Will. " Ecoutez. Connaissez-vous une dame qui s'appelle Madame Leyrisse? "

He had asked the question so often that it flowed off his tongue with the greatest of ease, and he had received a negative reply so often that he nearly fell off his chair with astonishment when the waiter nodded and smiled. But yes, of course he knew Madame Leyrisse. Did not his wife's cousin work in the garden at Villa des Cygnes?

Will gazed at the waiter; he was so amazed that he could not speak. He could not believe his ears. Was this really the end of his quest?

Meantime the waiter was chatting happily, for it was a quiet time in the little restaurant and he had nothing else to do—and this customer, who liked the wine of Nivennes, was English by the look of him—or possibly American—and therefore good for a decent tip—and, to tell the truth there was nothing the waiter enjoyed more than imparting information to anyone who would listen—and this customer was listening with breathless attention to every word he said.

But yes, of course he knew Madame Leyrisse, repeated the waiter. It would be strange indeed if he did not know her; Madame Leyrisse was well known in the town. She had lived for ten years or more at Villa des Cygnes and all that time, said the waiter, his wife's cousin had gone there every Saturday morning for two hours to keep the garden in order. It was not a large garden—that went without saying—but two hours a week was scarcely enough to keep it tidy. The waiter's wife's cousin had suggested three hours—but no, Madame Leyrisse said no quite firmly, and although she was so small and thin that one might think a puff of wind would blow her away she had a mind of her own. Yes indeed, Madame Leyrisse had a mind of her own, there was nobody in Nivennes who could drive a harder bargain. Lately she had been ill and had not been able to go about as usual and do her own marketing, but she had a daughter—a daughter who lived with her and looked after her with the greatest of care. How fortunate that was!

" The daughter——" began Will.

Ah yes, the daughter! The daughter of Madame Leyrisse was a different pair of shoes altogether. Perhaps Monsieur knew her? Perhaps Monsieur was aware of her so sad history? She had married an English soldier during the war and he had been killed a few weeks later —but that had happened before they came to Nivennes of course.

" Her name——" began Will, breathless with excitement.

The waiter shrugged his shoulders eloquently. He did not know her name . . . for that matter he doubted if anyone in Nivennes knew her name. Oh, there was no mystery about it—or none that he knew of—it was too difficult, that was all. In Nivennes the daughter of Madame Leyrisse was—just—the daughter of Madame Leyrisse. Voilà tout!

Will was silent.

Perhaps Monsieur would like to see her, suggested the waiter. This was market-day so if Monsieur would walk across to the market-place he would see the daughter of Madame Leyrisse with his own eyes.

Will explained that even if he saw her with his own eyes he would not know her, so it would be better to call at the house.

" Villa des Cygnes," nodded the waiter and added the information that the little house on the hill about two kilometres from the town.

A pourboire changed hands and Will got up.

" But stay! " cried the waiter, pursuing his customer to the door.

" Stay? " asked Will in surprise.

"It is an idea that has just occurred to me," explained the waiter, smiling from ear to ear. "Just this moment the idea has come—but that is the way of ideas. One moment the mind is a blank and the next moment the idea is born. No doubt Monsieur has discovered this himself?"

"Yes," agreed Will, hiding his amusement.

"Voilà," said the waiter eagerly. "It is a steep road to Villa des Cygnes—and the day is warm—it would be a very uncomfortable walk. Why undertake such an expedition when there is no need? If Monsieur so desires I will ask permission to go with Monsieur to the market and find the daughter of Madame Leyrisse. Nothing could be easier. She is sure to be there."

For a moment Will hesitated—things seemed to be moving very rapidly—then he nodded.

Five minutes later he was walking with the waiter in the sunshiny street.

Chapter 13

THE STREET had been full of colour but when Will and
his companion turned the corner into the wide square
where the market was being held the colours almost took
his breath away. There were stalls piled high with fruit
and vegetables, and others with flowers: roses, sweet
peas and carnations. There were stalls of farm produce:
pyramids of eggs; packets of butter, golden and creamy,
and rounds of cheese. Chickens and ducks hung
dangling, interspersed with sides of bacon and home-
cured hams. There were stalls of toys and sweets and
clothing of all kinds; there was a stall where you could
buy bottles of brightly-coloured drinks or boxes of pills,
or plasters for corns and bunions (and here a man with
a stentorian voice was shouting his wares). Each stall
had an awning; some were white, others were striped
red and yellow or pink and blue.

The sun beat down upon the scene in a glare of gold.
Will's eyes were dazed, his ears were deafened by the
noise and his nose was assailed by a mixture of smells—
some pleasant and recognisable, as the scent of flowers,
and others very curious indeed. The space round the
stalls was full of people of all sizes and ages and clothed
in all manner of dress. Some were loitering, others were
pushing through the crowd in a purposeful way, but all
were talking loudly and gesticulating wildly.

It seemed quite impossible that any one woman could be found amongst this throng. Will tried to say so to his companion but he could not make himself heard. He noticed, however, that his companion was smiling cheerfully and seemed quite undismayed.

" Monsieur must not get lost," shouted the waiter, seizing Will's arm. " Monsieur is not used to the market —and it is a little crowded to-day—but have no fear, I will find the daughter of Madame Leyrisse and bring her."

Will was left standing near a fruit-stall beside a lorry —a curiously shaped vehicle with spidery wheels—and after a parting injunction to wait there and not to move his companion pushed off amongst the seething crowd and disappeared.

By this time Will was so hot that his forehead was beaded with perspiration—perhaps it was not only the heat which had made him so hot! He took off his hat and mopped his face and sat down on a box to wait.

The fruit-stall belonged to a little fat man with a sallow face and after a few minutes this individual approached Will in an angry manner with a torrent of words which was quite incomprehensible, but it was obvious from his gestures that for some reason he objected to the stranger sitting upon his box. Will got up at once, for the last thing he wanted was to get involved in a brawl, whereupon the man moved the box to the back of the stall into the shade of the awning.

" Asseyez-vous," said the man in a rough coarse voice—and in answer to Will's thanks he muttered crossly that only an Englishman would be so foolish as to sit in the sunshine.

(I don't understand them at all, thought Will in perplexity. It isn't so much the language—though that's difficult enough—I just don't understand the way they tick.)

Here, at the back of the stall, it was not only cooler but less noisy. The crowds surged past but scarcely a creature glanced in Will's direction; they were far too intent upon their business of bargain-hunting to notice the stranger sitting upon the box.

Now that he was out of the turmoil and in comparative peace Will had time to look about him and to take in his surroundings. He noticed that the stall, though small, was very well set out. The fruit was beautiful, especially the apricots which looked perfect—ripe and juicy with pale golden skins. Indeed they looked so delicious that he decided to buy some and eat them here and now while he was waiting—and then he changed his mind. They would be very refreshing but at any moment the waiter might return with the lady, and it would be unfortunate to say the least of it if he were discovered in a juicy, sticky mess.

Will sat there for quite a long time—in fact he had almost given up hope—when a voice behind him exclaimed in triumphant tones:

" Voilà, Monsieur! La fille de Madame Leyrisse! "

A girl stood there looking at him. She was half in sunshine and half in the shadow of the awning. Unlike most of the women (who were dressed in black or some sort of dark colours) she was wearing a crisp white linen frock, sprigged with tiny flowers, and a wide straw hat. Beneath the shade of the hat her big dark eyes were shy —and frightened. Her red lips were parted a little and she was breathing quickly. Her skin was smooth as cream but of a deeper, warmer colour—it was almost the colour of the apricots which he had noticed on the stall.

Will rose quickly and took off his hat. They stood and looked at each other.

At first glance Will had thought she was a girl—quite young—but now he saw that she was older; probably about the same age as himself. Her figure was not slender, but neither was it plump, it was rounded in feminine curves. She was wearing no jewellery of any kind, no beads round her neck, no ear-rings, no jangly bracelets on her bare rounded arms . . . in fact her only "ornament" was the narrow golden band of her wedding ring.

All this Will saw in a few moments.

He had composed a sentence for this meeting, unfortunately he had forgotten it completely, but he had to say something. He began stumblingly, " Madame, vous êtes—Madame, pardonnez-moi——"

" I speak English," she said breathlessly. " I am Julie. You have been looking for me. I think you must be Rae's friend. I think you are Will." She was trembling all over as she spoke.

" Don't be frightened! " he exclaimed. " Yes, I'm Will—please come and sit down—it's all right, *really*—please don't be frightened! "

As she sat down she looked round anxiously and Will, following her glance, saw the boy who had been standing behind her; a boy of about eleven years old with long thin legs and honey-coloured hair, thick and tufty. His eyes which were raised to look at Will were very blue and set unusually far apart.

" Rae! " exclaimed Will involuntarily.

" Rae's son," said Julie. She said it sadly—almost as if she did not want to admit the fact.

" But—but I didn't know—but why——"

" Tom," said Julie. " You are to say how do you do—like Miss Vernon showed you. This gentleman and your father were friends. It is good to meet your father's friend. Tell him you are pleased."

" But of course I'm pleased! " exclaimed the boy, smiling up at Will and holding out his hand.

" Your hand is dirty," said his mother.

It certainly was dirty—and hot—and sticky—but Will did not mind. The years had rolled back and it seemed as if this were Rae himself whose hot, sticky hand he was holding.

" I speak English well," said Tom. " I am half English, you see. I speak much better than Maman."

" It is not good to be proud," said Julie reprovingly.

There was a moment's silence. Will was so overwhelmed that he could say nothing. He was afraid of saying the wrong thing.

" Tom," said Julie. " You will go home now and take the basket. You will say to Grandmaman that I have met an old friend and——"

" But, Maman—please! Can't I stay and talk to—to——"

" Not to-day. Another time perhaps——"

" But, Maman——"

" Not to-day."

" It would be so good for my English. Miss Vernon would like——"

" Go, Tom," said Tom's mother firmly.

131

Tom picked up the basket and went.

" I hope you will come and have lunch with me? " said Will, finding his voice with difficulty.

She nodded. "Yes, please. That would be nice. There is a lot to say."

2

There was so much to say that they did not know where to begin, and in any case it would have been difficult to talk about anything important as they pushed through the crowd. Will had forgotten the waiter, but now he remembered the man and explained this to his companion, adding that he must call at the little restaurant " and give him something."

" There is no need," replied Julie. " You have given him too much already—and it has been a nice little holiday for him to go to the market. We will not go to that café for lunch because it is always noisy and crowded. I will take you to another place."

She led the way to a tiny café on the other side of the street.

" They know me here," she said, looking up at Will and hesitating. " It is very small—as you see—but you will not mind? The food is good and there will be peace for us to talk."

Will followed her into a dark little cavern of a room, full of smoke and chatter and the clatter of plates and cutlery. They crossed the room, threading their way amongst the closely-packed tables, and opening another door found themselves on a veranda. There were vines overhead, shading it from the glare, and there were a few tables all of which were empty. A slope of sun-bleached grass ran down to a little stream.

" Will this be orlright? " asked Julie.

It was the first word she had pronounced wrongly. Her English was stilted but her accent was almost perfect. Will wondered where she had learned. " It's lovely here," he replied. " So cool and quiet."

" That is what I thought," agreed Julie. She pointed to a basket-chair and added, " Would you like to sit there? "

Already Julie had chosen a wooden chair with arms and had moved a table into a convenient place—Will had been too late to do it for her—and now she took off her hat and put it on a table nearby. Her hair was dark—smooth and shining—and gathered into a loose knot at the nape of her neck. Will had thought her very pretty and attractive, but now he saw she was beautiful, and in spite of the fact that she had spent the morning shopping in the market she looked as cool and fresh as a newly-picked flower. He thought vaguely, Yes, of course she would be—just like that. Not flimsy and frilly, with fuzzy hair and powder on her face, but just like that—beautiful and cool and natural.

" Madame," began Will, and paused uncertainly.

" Julie, please," she corrected with a little smile. " You are so well known to me. Rae spoke of you so much. He said, ' Will and I used to do that ' or ' One day when Will and I were fishing.' Oh, I know such a lot about ' Will '! And now I see you and it seems as if we had known each other before."

Will nodded. " Yes," he said rather huskily. " Yes,

133

we used to do everything together, Rae and I—and Patty."

It was at this moment that the waiter appeared to take their order. As a matter of fact Will was too upset to care what he had to eat, but to Julie it was obviously a very serious matter. She spoke to the man in rapid French and then said, " We could have an omelette with kidneys—would you like that, Will? Or we could have veal with little mushrooms and fried potatoes. It is more expensive but——"

" Let's have veal," said Will. " And some of that golden wine from the local vineyard—unless you would rather have something else."

" It would be nice," nodded Julie.

They agreed on that and ordered apricots and ice-cream and coffee to follow.

When the waiter had gone there was a little silence. There was so much Will wanted to know that he felt bewildered.

At last she sighed and said, " You are wondering things about me."

" All sorts of things," declared Will. " Why didn't Rae tell his family about you, Julie? "

" He tried to write a letter but it was too difficult. He was afraid his parents would not understand it properly. So then he laughed and tore it up into little pieces and said he would wait until he could go home and tell them. He said he could explain all about me and make things orlright."

Will nodded. There was such a charm about Rae that he could always " make things orlright."

" And—afterwards——" said Will, choosing his

words carefully. "Afterwards, Julie. Why didn't you write to Rae's father?"

"There were—reasons." She hesitated and then added, "I have been wondering all the time how you found me."

"You didn't want to be found?"

She shook her head.

"Why, Julie?"

"I was afraid," she replied as if that explained everything.

"Afraid!" he echoed in surprise.

"Because everything had gone," said Julie in a low voice. "Rae was killed; my brother was killed in the Resistance; my father died; we had to sell the farm. Our lives were broken in little pieces. It seemed better to go away to another place and try to begin another life. We had enough money to buy a little house, so we came to Nivennes and bought Villa des Cygnes. There is money for my mother and me to live on if we are very careful. It is possible to make a little extra with some sewing. We had each other, my mother and me. We had nothing else at all." Her lips were quivering. She turned her face away.

Will said gently, "I'm beginning to understand. But there was Tom, wasn't there?"

"Not then," she replied. "When we left Badlieu I did not know I would have a child. I never thought about it for a moment. There were so many other things to think about and I was so miserable and upset. When we left Badlieu there was just my mother and me. We wanted peace—and each other—that was all. We had been through so many troubles. We just wanted—peace."

135

" And you still want peace, Julie? " asked Will.

She raised her hands helplessly. " But I don't know what I want! "

" You're sorry I came and found you? "

" No, Will——" she began impulsively—and then she stopped.

" I very nearly didn't," Will told her. " I very nearly gave it up and went home. I'll tell you all about that later. We've got to decide what to do, haven't we? We've got to think of Tom. You want the best for Tom, don't you? "

" What mother does not want the best for her child? " exclaimed Julie. " Listen, Will, and I will try to tell you. At first it seemed to me that Tom was all mine—every little bit of him—but he grew from a baby and became a little boy and then I saw he belonged to Rae too. There is much of Rae in him, not only in his looks but in his character. He is bold and adventurous—like Rae. Our life here is very quiet and I can see that it is not very good for him. Soon he will want more—much more than I can give. You understand? "

Will nodded.

" Things happen strangely," continued Julie thoughtfully. " At first you think there is no pattern at all, and then you look back and you realise that there is—there is a pattern. Miss Vernon came to Nivennes."

" Miss Vernon? " asked Will, prompting her, for it was obvious that Miss Vernon—whoever she might be—was an important part of the pattern. As a matter of fact he had heard her name mentioned several times and had begun to feel curious about the lady.

" She came here because she was ill and must live in

a warm climate," Julie explained. " It is two years since we got to know her. She was sitting in the public gardens and she saw Tom playing with the other boys so she called him to speak to her. Tom does not look like the other boys in Nivennes. They talked together and Tom told her he was half English—he is proud of that. So then Miss Vernon wrote me a letter and asked if I would allow her to teach Tom to speak English. At first I said no, because my mother did not want it, but Tom wanted it so much that I went to see Miss Vernon and she made me see that it was right for Tom to learn to speak his father's language. I told her we could not pay for his lessons but she said there was no need to pay anything. She liked Tom and it would be a pleasure. She was very kind and nice—and I think she was lonely. So Tom went to her apartment every day after school and she gave him lessons. Later when I got to know her better I had lessons too. I think I was a little bit jealous," said Julie frankly. " I was jealous that Tom should learn English and not me. I did not think of it at the time, but now I think that was the reason. Sometimes we do not understand our own hearts."

" You both speak wonderfully well."

" Miss Vernon says Tom speaks much better than me —and of course it is true—but it is not good for him to be proud."

" Children learn languages more easily."

" Yes, Tom can think in English and he has learnt to run his words together quickly—like an English boy."

" Very nearly like an English boy," agreed Will. As a matter of fact Tom spoke more like an English lady than an English boy, but that was only natural under the circumstances.

" I have often wished I could give Miss Vernon a present," said Julie with a sigh. " She has been so kind and patient——"

" What would you like to give her? "

" A radiogram," said Julie without a moment's hesitation. " She is so musical. It would be lovely for her. I have often thought if I had a lot of money I would give Miss Vernon a radiogram for her birthday. It would make her so happy."

" We'll get one for her," said Will, nodding understandingly.

Julie gazed at him in amazement. " Get one—for her! "

" Why not? I mean if that's what she would like."

" You mean it—seriously? It is not a joke? You would give Miss Vernon a radiogram? "

" You would give it to her of course. I mean I'll pay for it and you'll give it to her—see? "

" But, Will, that would not be right! " cried Julie. " It would be—it would be so strange. I never thought of that when I spoke of a present for Miss Vernon—and you do not even know her! "

" You know her. She has been kind to you and Tom."

" A radiogram would be very, very expensive. You must be very rich to think of it," declared Julie. " But I could not let you do it all the same."

Will could not help smiling a little. He said, " No, I'm not ' very rich ' but I can easily afford to buy a radiogram for you to give your friend."

" Why should you? I don't understand——"

"Why shouldn't I, Julie? It's nothing. Rae and I were like brothers. We shared everything. I would have done anything for Rae. I would have shared my last crust with Rae. Please try to understand, Julie."

She said softly, "I think I have been—very stupid."

"Well, that's settled then," said Will. It was a minor matter but he had won his point. He only hoped and prayed that all the other matters, so much more important, could be settled as easily.

3

Afterwards when Will looked back upon this first conversation with Julie he was to see it as a picture in his mind; the shady veranda with the thin white pillars; the golden glare of the sunshine sparkling upon the little stream, striking through the vine-leaves overhead and making little patterns upon the tiled floor and the white tablecloth . . . and Julie herself with her smooth velvety skin and dark hair and big brown eyes.

They talked about many things. Will told her about the letter which Patty had shown him, and all about his "wild-goose chase." She smiled at that and the dimples in her cheeks came and went in a most attractive manner. ("I am the wild goose?" she asked. "That is not very polite of you, Will. But, yes, I am very often a goose.")

He was glad to see she was losing her fear of him for he had realised that the best way to gain his ends was to make friends with Julie. If she trusted him she would be more likely to come with him to Langford and bring Tom. She must do this sooner or later—but the sooner the better. At the beginning of their talk she had said she wanted the best for Tom and now Will was wondering how to lead back naturally to the discussion of plans for the future . . . but after all they returned to it naturally, so he need not have worried.

Will had been telling her of his " adventures " and bewailing the fact that he found it so difficult to express his feelings in French.

" It is difficult to talk in a foreign language," agreed Julie. " I can talk English now, but when Rae and I were married I could not talk to him at all in his own tongue. It would have been nice," she added with a little sigh.

" Rae spoke French——"

" Oh yes, he spoke well; it was no bother to him. It amused him to teach me how to say things in English. We talked and talked. There was so much to say and so little time to say it. Sometimes we talked all night and when the morning came we were still talking." Her eyes were shining with unshed tears which hung on her long dark lashes. " We were very happy," she whispered. " It was not long—but it was good and beautiful—to be married to Rae."

" I'm glad! " exclaimed Will impulsively. It comforted him to know that Rae had snatched a brief spell of happiness in the midst of the horrors of war. " They will be glad too," he added without thinking.

" They? " she asked in surprise.

" I mean Rae's parents. You'll come and see them, won't you, Julie? "

" Will they want me to come? "

" Yes of course. They'll want to hear all you can tell them about Rae. They'll want to see Tom."

She looked at him pitifully. The fear had come back into her eyes.

"Don't be frightened," said Will quickly. "They won't want to take Tom away from you—just to share him."

"But that is the trouble! He cannot be shared. You have not thought of this like me or you would not say it. I have thought of this for years. Think of it now, Will! Think of it seriously and you will see he cannot be shared. Oh, Will, what am I to do!"

Will hesitated and then he said, "Langford is a beautiful place and some day it will belong to Tom."

"I was not sure——"

"Yes, it will belong to Tom. Julie, listen, it really is—beautiful. The old house is near the river; there are trees all round it. There are farms on the estate. There are moors with heather. Rae loved riding over the moors. Rae loved every inch of his home."

"Yes, I know," said Julie in a quivering voice. "He talked about it—to me."

"Julie," said Will very gently. "Rae would want you to see Langford. He would want his son to go home. You know that, don't you?"

She did not reply. Her tears overflowed and she put her hands over her face and gave a little sob. She had come to the end of her strength and could bear no more.

Chapter 14

IT WAS the morning after his meeting with Julie; Will
was having his breakfast of coffee and rolls in his bedroom at the hotel. The waiter had brought it and dumped
the tray down upon the table without a word; he had
not even had the decency to say, " Bon jour." Will
wondered if this was the waiter's usual demeanour or if
the man disliked him intensely—but, if so, why? The
problem was unsolvable—and the coffee was cooling—
so Will gave up the struggle and got on with his meal,
thinking somewhat nostalgically of his father sitting
down to porridge and bacon and eggs in the dining-room
at Broadmeadows.

Angry voices in the yard outside his window disturbed
Will's thoughts and brought him back in the twinkling
of an eye from Broadmeadows to Nivennes. There was
a man's voice, shouting furiously, and a boy's voice
replying with equal vigour. What they were saying was
quite unintelligible but it sounded like a first-class row.
Will had neither dressed nor shaved for it was still early,
but the disturbance aroused his curiosity so he stepped
out on to the balcony and leaning over the balustrade
looked down.

The yard was large and paved with cobbles and sur
rounded by tumble-down buildings which had once

been stables. It seemed that the disturbance was almost over; the disagreeable waiter had a small boy by the collar and was dragging him towards the wooden gates. The boy was being ejected, that was obvious, and he was not taking his ejection meekly (he was yelling like mad and squirming like an eel) but the waiter was a big burly type; he hurled the boy into the road and shut and barred the gates. Then he dusted his hands together and returned to his duties muttering angrily.

It was rather an amusing incident; Will wished he had seen the beginning of it, he also wished he could understand the language. What had the boy done to be thrown out so savagely? Stealing something most likely and caught in the act. What a lot I'm missing! thought Will regretfully as he stepped back into his bedroom to finish his last cup of tepid coffee.

Five minutes later a head appeared at his window in a somewhat stealthy manner and a voice exclaimed triumphantly " Oh good! It's you! I wasn't quite sure if it was you looking over the balcony so I had to be careful."

" Tom! " cried Will in amazement.

" Yes, it's me," declared Tom, laughing delightedly. " Did you see what happened? I got the better of the garçon, didn't I? "

" I thought he got the better of you," replied Will, smiling.

" Oh no, he didn't. He threw me out—the fat stupid pig—but I'm in."

Certainly Tom was in, for by this time he was sitting cross-legged on the end of Will's bed and grinning . . .

and he was so like Rae—a triumphant Rae who had been successful in some especially difficult piece of mischief —that Will's heart gave an uncomfortable leap.

" He threw me out," repeated Tom. " But he couldn't *keep* me out. I climbed on to the roof of a shed and from thence to the balcony—and behold me! "

Will beheld him with pleasure for to tell the truth he had been somewhat anxious lest a boy brought up by a doting mother might be a bit of a milksop.

" I wished to see you," added Tom with sudden gravity.

This was obvious, of course.

" Why did he throw you out? " asked Will.

" He said it was too early. He said you hadn't finished le petit déjeuner and wouldn't want to see me."

" Was that all? " Will inquired, for it seemed to him that if no crime had been committed the waiter had used unnecessary violence.

" That was all—except that I was a little rude to him. I was annoyed, you see. It was important that I should see you early. I wished to see you shaving."

" To see me shaving! "

" I live with two ladies," explained Tom.

Will nodded; he took the point. He realised that it was rather comical but he did not feel like smiling, for he remembered that when he himself was a little boy he had enjoyed watching his father shave—and this was Rae's son who "lived with two ladies." No, Will did not feel like smiling.

2

Will had begun his daily task and was explaining its mysteries to his visitor when the waiter appeared to remove the breakfast tray. The waiter barged into the room in his usual uncouth manner—and then stopped dead in his tracks, for, lo and behold, there was his victim (whom he had thrown out of the gates so ignominiously) sitting upon the bed perfectly at ease.

" Me voiçi! " said Tom cheerfully.

The waiter was dumb with astonishment and before he had time to recover Tom said a great deal more with a wealth of gesture and a rapid flow of language which would have put to shame an orange-box orator at Hyde Park Corner.

Will watched the man's face and wondered what Tom was saying (he would have given a lot to know). Rage and astonishment gave way to doubt and consternation. Once or twice the man made an attempt to interrupt the tirade but without success. The man was talked down: he was completely cowed; he was dispatched with a wave of Tom's hand. He picked up the tray and departed hastily, closing the door with his foot.

" There," said Tom complacently. " I have given him a lesson he won't forget in a hurry. He's frightened."

" Yes, I could see he was frightened. What on earth did you say? "

" Oh, didn't you understand? " asked Tom in surprise. " I told him you were an English lord with a big property and great wealth."

" But I'm not! "

"Maman says you are. Maman says your property is almost as large as mine, and it is next door to mine. We are neighbours. Our estates march—that's the right way to say it."

"Yes," agreed Will. "But Langford doesn't belong to you yet, you know, nor Broadmeadows to me."

"They will—later," said Tom airily. "There's no hurry about it. I have no wish for my grandfather to die before his time . . . but it wasn't necessary to explain these details to the garçon."

"But, Tom——"

"Soyez tranquille," said Tom. "I know these canaille. You will receive better service."

Will was not so sure. He said somewhat anxiously, "You told him a great deal more than that."

"Oh yes," agreed Tom. "I told him all about you. I told him you had farms on your estate with cows and sheep in them and high hills for hunting pheasants and a river in which to catch fish. I said you had horses to ride on and a great many servants, and if one of your servants appeared before you in a dirty apron you would dismiss him at once—his apron was very dirty indeed. I said you were quite disgusted with this miserable hotel and intended to complain about the wretched breakfast. Everyone knows that English lords have bacon and eggs for breakfast—everyone except ignorant pigs like him. I think that was all," added Tom, wrinkling his brows in an effort to remember.

When Will had finished laughing and could speak, he said, "But, Tom, you haven't ordered another breakfast, have you?"

146

" There was no need to order it. He has gone to get it in a great hurry—as you saw."

" But I've had breakfast——"

" Don't worry," said Tom kindly. " My adventures have given me an appetite and I like bacon and eggs."

" Tom, you'll kill me! " gasped Will, holding his sides in an agony of mirth.

3

Madame Leyrisse had sent Will a message to say she would like to see him; he was invited to lunch at Villa des Cygnes. Will was not very anxious to go, but it was impossible to refuse, so he set off up the hill as directed and arrived at the Villa in good time. It was a neat little house—scarcely more than a cottage—with a well-grown hedge and a tiny garden full of flowers which did credit to the waiter's wife's cousin who tended it once a week.

Remembering this, Will was reminded of what the waiter had said about Madame Leyrisse; she was so small and thin that one might think a puff of wind would blow her away but nobody in Nivennes could drive a harder bargain. The description was not attractive and he wished he had not remembered it just at this moment; however, it could not be helped. Julie had seen him coming and opened the door and received him in a very friendly manner.

" My mother is looking forward to meeting you," she said, adding in a low voice, " My mother does not understand English so we must speak in French all the time —and it is better that I call you Monsieur Hastie—and

I have not told her about Tom's little visit to you this morning nor about the present you are going to give Miss Vernon. It will be better not to speak of Miss Vernon at all because my mother does not like her——"

Will was about to say he would be discreet but by this time they were in the hall and Madame Leyrisse appeared from the back premises.

"What are you telling Monsieur 'Astee?" she inquired suspiciously.

"I told him you had been looking forward to meeting him," replied Julie without a moment's hesitation.

They had spoken in French, of course, but they spoke clearly and Will was relieved to find that he could understand what they said. He saw at once that the waiter's description of Madame Leyrisse was apt, she looked fragile but her small sallow face was hard and her beady eyes were shrewd and unfriendly.

Very little time was wasted in introductions, for lunch was already on the table. The three of them went in and sat down. Julie explained that Tom was at school and it was too far for him to come home.

In spite of the fact that the food was excellent, his lunch at Villa des Cygnes was one of the most unpleasant meals Will had ever endured. He did his best to speak to his hostess but every word he had ever known went out of his head. There was little need for "discretion"; he was unable to make the simplest remark without stumbling and stuttering like an idiot.

Madame Leyrisse did not attempt to help him; she sat and stared at him with her beady eyes.

"It is difficult for Monsieur Hastie," said Julie. "It is a long time since he has spoken French."

"I cannot understand one word he is saying. His accent is atrocious," declared Madame Leyrisse.

"Oh, Maman!" cried Julie in dismay.

"You had better tell me what he means—if it is worth translating," added Madame Leyrisse scornfully.

It was not worth translating, of course. Will had merely endeavoured to say that the flowers in the garden of Villa des Cygnes were very pretty.

When the futile remark was translated to her Madame Leyrisse exclaimed, "Does he think I am blind?"

After that it was useless for Will to try to say anything, so he was silent except for an occasional "Oui" or "Non" in reply to poor Julie's gallant attempts at conversation.

Madame Leyrisse was his enemy. The sheer hatred which lurked in her beady eyes was positively alarming. Will had never been hated before—not hated like this, personally, inexorably, maliciously. He would have got up and left the table if it had not been for Julie . . . but for Julie's sake he was obliged to bear it, to eat the food —which stuck in his gullet—and pretend all was well.

4

At last the meal was over and Will was able to escape. Julie went with him to the gate.

"Oh, Will, I am sorry!" she exclaimed. "I made a mistake when I asked you to come and see my mother. It was dreadful for you."

"She—she dislikes me."

"It is not you, yourself," declared Julie. "She would dislike anyone who wanted to take us away."

"Yes, I see that, but you'll come, won't you?"

"It will be difficult——"

"Oh, Julie, please! Promise me you'll come. They're so sad and it would give them so much pleasure. Oh, Julie, if you could see how sad they are——"

"Sad because of Rae?"

Will nodded. "Yes, his mother is still waiting for him to come home. She talks of him constantly."

"She is mad?"

"Yes—I suppose she is—really," admitted Will with reluctance.

They were silent for a few moments, leaning on the gate. It was pleasant here after the stuffy room, pleasant and peaceful; the sun was warm but Villa des Cygnes stood high and there was a little breeze. The view was wide and varied, you could see the town lying in the valley—a clean little town with white-washed houses and red-tiled roofs. Some of the houses had been "white-washed" in pale pink or pale blue, which made a pleasant contrast. The silver-grey of the olive trees and the built-up terraces of the vineyard were on the hill beyond.

At last Julie said, "And Rae's father? Do you think he will like Tom?"

"He'll love Tom dearly. Nobody could help loving Tom."

Her face brightened. She looked up at Will and smiled.

"But it isn't only that," continued Will. "He'll be so happy to have his grandson as his heir. Langford is entailed, which means the Colonel can't leave it to Patty —or to anybody he likes. Langford would have gone to a nephew—that's what we thought would happen. But now it will belong to Tom," added Will in joyful accents.

" The nephew is not a nice person? " asked Julie shrewdly.

" Not nice at all," replied Will with conviction.

" The nephew will be angry? "

" He'll be as sick as mud," declared Will with unholy glee.

Julie smiled, and her dimples came and went in the usual delightful manner. " Sick as mud," she repeated. It was obvious that the expression was new to her; she had not learnt it from Miss Vernon.

" Gosh! " exclaimed Will. " I just wish I could be there when he hears about Tom! I'd give almost anything to be there—and see his face."

" He must be a very horrible person," said Julie, laughing.

" Very horrible indeed."

" What has he done? " inquired Julie with interest. " I mean what has he done that is so wicked? "

" Oh well," said Will, thinking over the various crimes which Hugo had committed and wondering which of them to retail. " Oh well, he—er—he talks too much for one thing, and his hair is far too long—and curly—and—and——"

Julie nodded gravely. " His sins are too bad to tell me. I can see that."

Will hesitated for a moment, but it was impossible to explain so he was obliged to leave it alone.

" Well, anyhow," said Will. " You can take it from me that Hugo is an absolute rotter which makes it even more important that you and Tom should come to Langford."

"I have said we will come. I said that before when we were talking about it, Will. But it need not be for a long time——"

"It must be soon," he declared. "Honestly, Julie, there are all sorts of reasons. Rae's parents are old and very frail. That's one reason. Another reason, even more important, is Tom himself. Tom must grow up at Langford."

"Grow up at Langford?" asked Julie in dismay.

"Oh, Julie, don't you see?" exclaimed Will desperately. "How can I make you understand? Turn it back to front. Look at that vineyard over there on the hill. Whom does it belong to?"

"André Delormes," replied Julie in bewilderment. "It belonged to his father, and now it belongs to him —but I don't see——"

"And when he dies it will belong to his son?"

"But he is not married!"

"He'll get married some day, and he'll have a son," declared Will. "Let's suppose so, anyway. The son will grow up here in Nivennes and learn all about vines —all about how to look after them and how to make that golden wine. André Delormes wouldn't want his son to be brought up in England and to come here as a stranger; not knowing anything about the business, not knowing anything about the people on the estate. That wouldn't be a good thing at all, would it, Julie?"

For a few moments Julie was silent and then she said, "That is what you mean by turning it back to front."

Will nodded, "It's a thing I do about problems,"

he explained. "Perhaps it's a bit silly but it often works."

"It has worked," said Julie sadly.

There was no need to say more. Julie's hand was gripping the top bar of the gate, so Will put his hand over it and gave it a little squeeze. She did not seem to mind.

Chapter 15

DURING THE next few days Will and Julie met several times to talk things over. They met in the town and sat on a seat in the public gardens, and on one occasion they walked along the path beside the stream. They talked about many things.

Julie had agreed to come to Langford and bring Tom but she could not name a date. Madame Leyrisse was using all her influence to persuade Julie not to go to Langford at all and her influence was strong. (The influence which French parents exert over their sons and daughters is very strong indeed.) Julie was no weakling but she was pulled this way and that. When she was with Will she saw quite clearly that her duty was to go, but when she was with her mother she became less sure about it. Was not one's first duty to take care of an ailing mother?

"Come soon," urged Will. "Come for a short visit."

" A short visit? Would that be any good? " asked Julie doubtfully.

Will thought it would. At any rate it would be a beginning. It would be the thin edge of the wedge. Once they had come and seen Langford, and the Elliot Murrays had seen *them*, the affair would be out of Will's hands and he would not feel burdened with responsibilities. They could make their own plans for the future. Will did not say all this to Julie, it was better not to, he just said, " Yes, come for a short visit. Come with me. We'll go next week——"

" Next week! " exclaimed Julie in dismay. " But there are a hundred arrangements to be made. I must find somebody nice to look after my mother! I must buy clothes——"

" She would be all right for a short time, wouldn't she? We'll fly," said Will earnestly. " We'll all fly home together as soon as I can book seats on a plane."

" But that is impossible! You have not told them about us. Am I to appear without warning on the doorstep of Rae's father? It is unthinkable—surely you must see that? "

" Come to Broadmeadows."

" To your father's house? "

" Yes, he would be delighted to have you."

" But that would be almost the same as the doorstep of Rae's father! "

It would be, of course—Will saw that—but all the same he did not want to go home without them. He had found them with the greatest difficulty and he was reluctant to take his eyes off them until he had delivered them safely to Langford. Madame Leyrisse was sly and unscrupulous; he did not see what she could do, exactly, but he had no doubt she would do all she could by fair means or foul to keep them in her grasp.

He could have written to Colonel Elliot Murray—and indeed this seemed the obvious thing to do—but when he sat down to the task he found himself at a loss. How could he explain the whole story? The very beginning of the story was inexplicable; it had all started from the hint in Rae's last letter to Patty and he could not mention the letter without Patty's consent. Will wasted sheets of writing-paper before he gave up the task in despair.

In spite of the difficulties and the problem which nagged at his mind (and which could not be solved even by his usual almost infallible method of turning it back to front), Will was not by any means unhappy, for he felt he was gaining ground. Already he had won Tom's heart. Tom appeared every morning on his way to school and sat on the bed and watched Will shaving and shared his meal of bacon and eggs. Tom wanted to know all about Langford and Will was only too pleased to tell him. There was no doubt at all in Tom's mind about whether or not he was coming to Langford—and coming soon.

" Is it very difficult to ride on a horse? " he inquired.

" Not a bit," declared Will. " Your grandfather will get you a quiet pony and I'll teach you to ride."

" Yes," said Tom with a smile of anticipation. " And you'll teach me to shoot and catch fish and do all the things my father used to do, won't you, Will? "

(Tom had been requested to use this form of address to his new friend, for as a matter of fact his new friend found it natural and pleasant. To be addressed in a more formal manner by anybody who looked so like Rae seemed most unnatural and distinctly unpleasant.)

" You'll learn everything," promised Will as he lathered his face. " That's why I want you and Maman to come soon. It's easy to learn things when you're ten. Difficult when you're older."

" We'll come soon," agreed Tom. " Maman wants

to. It's Grandmaman that keeps on talking and talking and making it difficult."

Will had known this already.

Tom had been easily won and Julie was " coming round " rapidly. Every time they met they seemed to understand each other better. She was a delightful creature, so beautiful to look at, so sweet-natured and unselfish, so full of fun. Will enjoyed making her smile and watching her dimples come and go; it was not difficult, he found, to make Julie smile.

He had set out to make friends with Julie so that she would learn to trust him and would come with him to Langford but he soon forgot about this ulterior motive and enjoyed her company for her own sake.

2

On the third day Julie failed to turn up at the appointed rendezvous, and Will, after waiting for an hour, returned to the hotel disappointed and distressed. It was impossible to find out what had happened for Villa des Cygnes was not on the telephone and he could not call at the villa because of Madame Leyrisse. He wondered if Julie were ill—or perhaps some accident had befallen Tom and Julie was unable to leave him. Tom was bold and adventurous, he was fond of climbing trees or walls or roofs. He had boasted that he never walked home up the hill but ran after cars or vans and hung on behind and was carried to his destination without fatigue. Tom could easily have fallen or got run over!

Will spent a restless and miserable night imagining all sorts of frightful disasters, and wondering what he should do . . . but he had worried quite unnecessarily for the next morning Tom appeared at his window at the usual hour and in his usual robust state of health.

" Oh, Maman isn't ill," said Tom in answer to Will's anxious inquiries. " It's Grandmaman that's ill."

This news relieved Will's mind considerably.

" At least she *said* she was ill," continued Tom. " She said she would die if Maman left her. She said she was giddy and she got up out of bed and staggered about like this——" and Tom gave a realistic performance of his grandmother's condition, staggering round Will's bedroom, holding his head and groaning pitifully. The performance ended abruptly with two back somersaults and a handstand.

" Grandmaman didn't do that, did she?" asked Will in surprise.

" No, she didn't," replied Tom, giggling and smoothing down his tufty hair. "I just felt like it—suddenly."

It was obvious that Tom was not in the least upset about Grandmaman's illness, but children are seldom sympathetic towards people they are not fond of—and who could be fond of that old gargoyle? Will remembered his own childhood. He remembered that he and Rae had been jubilant when one of the keepers on the Langford estate had been taken ill and removed to hospital on a stretcher. They had disliked the man intensely (he was " a sneak ") and they had wondered hopefully if he would die. Even the tender-hearted Patty, who had been known to shed tears over the demise of a mouse, had said quite cheerfully that at any rate he would be ill for a long time; she had heard the parents discussing the matter and a new keeper was being engaged.

So Will acquitted Tom of being unnaturally callous
and they sat down together to enjoy their bacon and
eggs.

The disagreeable waiter was disagreeable no longer—
in fact since Tom's lesson Will had found him embar-
rassingly attentive. This had surprised Will considerably;
he could not understand it at all. If you had " walked
into " a Scotsman like that, had raged and stormed at
him and had told him all those fairy tales, the Scotsman
would have reacted in quite a different manner. It just
showed the difference, thought Will. It showed how
impossible it was to deal with people unless you were
used to them and understood them inside out. Carrying
this idea to its logical conclusion, Will realised how very
important it was that Tom should come home to Langford as soon as possible and learn to understand his
own people.

He tried to explain this to Tom.

" Oh yes," agreed Tom. " But he saw you arrive.
He saw you walk into the hotel with a knapsack on your
back so he didn't know you were an important person
until I told him. If you had arrived in a big automobile
with a great deal of luggage he would have been nice
to you from the beginning."

This was not what Will meant, but he had to leave it.

Unfortunately Tom could not stay this morning to see
Will shaving. He explained that he had been late for
school three days running and, having used up all the
excuses he could think of, he would get into serious
trouble if he were late again. He departed by the balcony,
for although he could now walk in at the door without

let or hindrance he preferred the more adventurous mode of entrance and exit to Will's room.

" Goodbye, Will," he said. " I'll see you to-morrow. Oh, I nearly forgot to tell you! Maman said she would meet you at the café at twelve o'clock."

" Did she say——"

" Yes, but you needn't bother because I'm sure Grandmaman won't let her come. Grandmaman hates you," added Tom cheerfully—and so saying he vanished.

Chapter 16

In spite of Tom's advice Will turned up at the café
much too early and sat down on the veranda to wait.
He hoped Julie would come, but if she did not come
he had made up his mind to call at the villa and see her.
Presumably Madame Leyrisse was in bed—or staggering about her bedroom—so it would be perfectly safe
to call . . . and he *must* see Julie to-day for on leaving
the hotel he had been handed a letter from his father
which had distressed him considerably.

Things were going badly at Langford, said Mr.
Hastie. The Colonel was in a very low state of mind.
He did not complain, of course—it was not his way to
complain—but it was obvious that he was terribly upset
about the broken engagement. He had been hoping
that Patty would marry Hugo and have a son to inherit
Langford. It had been his dearest wish. Mr. Hastie
had been to see him and found him very unhappy. He
had confided to his old friend that he felt tired; too tired
to go out for his usual saunter on the hill, too tired to
read . . . and he was worried about what would happen
to his wife and daughter when he had gone. Hugo
would not consider them—that was certain—they would

be turned out of Langford, and where were they to go? Mr. Hastie had done his best to comfort and cheer him but with little success. As for Patty, she was miserable; she felt it was all her fault, poor girl.

Rereading the letter Will saw that he must fly home with all speed, for the news that there was a ready-made grandson to inherit Langford was just the right tonic for Colonel Elliot Murray. Not only would it cheer him and give him an interest in life but it would allay his fears for the future. Yes, he must fly home on the first plane he could get. If Julie and Tom could not go with him he must go alone and come back for them later. It was a pity, but it could not be helped.

Will had just reached this decision when he saw Julie; she had come the back way by the path along the stream and was approaching the veranda up the slope. She was wearing white to-day—a perfectly plain white frock which she had probably made herself—and was carrying her hat in her hand. The sun shone upon her smooth dark head and golden skin but that did not trouble her; Julie loved the sunshine. She was a child of the sun— she basked in heat that would have given most people sunstroke.

" Oh, Julie! " cried Will, rising to meet her. " I was so afraid you weren't coming. This is lovely! You can stay and have lunch, can't you? " He took her hand and kissed it.

" That is not an English custom, Will," said Julie, smiling.

" No, but it's French. When you're in Rome you should do as the Romans do. Besides, I wanted to do it."

" Two good reasons," admitted Julie. She added,

"Yes, I can stay for half an hour, but not any longer. The wife of the gardener is a kind woman and will take care of Maman till I go home."

"I'm sorry your mother is ill."

"It is her nerves. She suffers terribly from her nerves, and the fear that we may leave her and go away has upset her and made her ill. I could not come yesterday, it was impossible. You were not cross with me, Will?"

"Not cross," he replied, smiling at the word. "I was just frightened and worried to death. I imagined all sorts of horrible disasters . . . but never mind. You're all right, that's the main thing."

They ordered lunch. It was almost the same as the first day they had had their meal together, but not quite. They knew each other now; there was no constraint between them; they could talk like old friends. Will read aloud his father's letter and Julie agreed that he must go home immediately.

"I shall miss you," she said regretfully. "It has been so nice—but you must go home and comfort Rae's father."

"I'll tell him you'll come soon and bring Tom."

"Yes, for a little visit—tell him that. Then we can make plans together; that is the best way." She hesitated and smiled a trifle sadly and then continued. "You have made Tom want to go to Langford—it was rather naughty of you, Will, and it was very naughty to make him late for school. The headmaster is as sick as mud."

Will burst out laughing, he could not help it.

"Have I said a wrong thing?" asked Julie in surprise.

"Not wrong," gasped Will. "It just sounded—so funny—that's all———"

" You said it about that terribly wicked man," said Julie, smiling. " You taught me to say it—that is another naughty thing you have done. I think you are almost as wicked as Hugo."

Will passed over this frightful insult with a smile. " I didn't intend to do all these wicked things. Honestly, Julie."

" But you have done them. Tom is to have a horse to ride on when he goes to Langford, and a little gun of his very own to shoot with, and you will teach him to catch fish in the river."

" Yes, but all that will be quite natural for a boy in his position—all that and much more. You understand don't you? "

" Yes, I understand," admitted Julie with a sigh.

They had finished lunch by this time and Julie was obliged to go. She had stayed much longer than she had intended.

Will took her hand and said earnestly, " Julie, listen, I'm going away because I have to, but I'll come back and fetch you whenever you give the word. You've promised to come, haven't you? "

" I have promised two or three or four times. What else can I say? "

" And you'll write to me, won't you? Write and tell me what you're doing—and all about Tom—and everything."

" Yes," said Julie. " I will write. It will not be a good letter at all. There will be a lot of stupid mistakes in the letter—but perhaps you will not mind."

2

When Will returned to the hotel after his parting with Julie he was told at the desk that a lady had called to see him and was waiting in the lounge. The news surprised him considerably and he wondered who on earth she could be. The thought passed through his mind that it might be Madame Leyrisse risen from her bed of sickness—and this was such a dreadful thought that Will hesitated at the door before going in. But it was no good hesitating so he plucked up his courage and went in boldly.

A woman whom Will had never seen before was the only occupant of the lounge; she was reading a newspaper, so Will had time to take a good look at her. She was very thin with a straight nose and greying hair, the hands which were holding the newspaper were long and narrow. The newspaper was French but the lady was English—Will knew that at once. If he had seen her in the most unlikely place, in Spain or Constantinople, in Greenland or darkest Africa, he would have known she was " an English spinster of uncertain age."

The unknown lady got up when she saw Will and came forward smiling and holding out her hand. " I'm Adela Vernon," she said. " I've heard so much about you, and I expect you've heard a good deal about me."

They shook hands and laughed.

Will's laugh was partly relief. " Perhaps you'd like tea? " he said. It was his instant reaction to the appearance of his visitor.

" Tea! " she exclaimed in surprise. " Have you for-

gotten where you are, Major Hastie? You can't get tea
here——"

" I can," said Will a trifle smugly. " I can get tea.
I can get anything I want in this hotel. I can even get
bacon and eggs for breakfast—thanks to Tom! "

" Thanks to Tom? "

" Yes, I'll tell you about that later. Let's order tea
first, shall we? "

When tea had been ordered they sat down together
for a talk.

" We owe you a lot——" began Will.

" You owe me nothing," declared Miss Vernon. " It
has been the greatest pleasure to teach them English.
They're both darlings—and extremely intelligent. That's
what I came about, really. You mustn't think of giving
me a radiogram. I don't deserve it."

Will did not answer that directly. He said, " The
Elliot Murrays will bless you for what you've done.
Everything would have been a thousand times more
difficult if it hadn't been for you."

" I see that, of course," she admitted. " Only a fool
could fail to see it. As a matter of fact I've seen it all
along."

" You've seen it all along? "

" From the very first day when I spoke to Tom in
the gardens," nodded Miss Vernon. She hesitated and
then continued, " I must admit that at first I didn't
believe all he told me—I thought he was making it up—
all about his father, and the estate in Scotland and—
and——"

" And the hills for hunting pheasants," suggested
Will.

"Yes—all that," agreed Miss Vernon, smiling. "It sounded like a fairy tale to me. So I wrote to a friend in London and asked her to make some tactful inquiries about the Elliot Murrays and I found it was all true. It was difficult to know what to do about it."

Will was silent.

"I see you blame me," said Miss Vernon with a sigh. "But honestly, Major Hastie, what *was* I to do? I spoke to Julie, of course. I told her she ought to get in touch with her husband's people, but she wouldn't hear of it. Could I have written to them behind her back? Perhaps I was wrong, but I just couldn't do it. I saw what it would mean: she would lose Tom—and Tom is the light of her eyes. Tom will have to go to Scotland. That's what it means, doesn't it?"

"Yes, but he's the heir, Miss Vernon, and if I hadn't found them quite by accident——"

"You would have heard," interrupted Miss Vernon. "Oh, I'm not such a fool! I had made up my mind to hold a watching brief, to wait until Tom was twelve years old and if nothing happened before that to write to Colonel Elliot Murray and tell him the whole story . . . and to make things perfectly safe I wrote a letter and sealed it and sent it to my lawyer in London to be delivered to Colonel Elliot Murray on my death."

"Yes," said Will thoughtfully. "Yes, I see—but ——"

"Meanwhile I taught Tom to speak English," Miss Vernon pointed out.

"Yes," agreed Will. "But, supposing——"

"To be quite frank I thought of another possibility,"

admitted Miss Vernon. "Julie is a very attractive
creature and I hoped she might marry again. That's
what I meant when I said 'if nothing happened.' Of
course if *that* had happened it would have been plain
sailing. She could have parted with Tom more easily.
It wouldn't have broken her heart."

"You seem to have thought of every possible contingency!"

"Except what has happened. I never thought of that.
But that's life, isn't it, Major Hastie?"

Will nodded; it was true. (You thought of everything that could possibly happen, and then something
happened that you had never thought of!) Aloud he
said, "But Julie can come too. The Elliot Murrays
will be only too delighted to have her; she won't have
to part with Tom."

"I doubt if she will leave her mother—and it isn't a
very happy thing to be an exile. I can tell you that from
experience. There's a queer pull. There's a horrible
loneliness——"

She quoted in a low voice:

> "*I travell'd among unknown men,*
> "*In lands beyond the sea;*
> "*Nor, England! did I know till then*
> "*What love I bore to thee.*"

"Cheers!" exclaimed Will. "That's my poem! It's
been haunting me! It's the one I remembered the day
after I got home—but I could only remember the first
two lines and I didn't know who it was by."

"Wordsworth," said Miss Vernon, smiling at his
excitement. She added, "You can substitute 'Scotland'

if you like. It's a poem especially designed for every lonely exile under the sun."

Will realised she was thinking of Julie. "But—just supposing she married—somebody in Scotland? Just supposing——"

"That's another contingency I never thought of," admitted Miss Vernon gravely. "Just supposing *that* happened—I should like to be asked to the wedding."

Nothing more of importance was said. They talked about other things while they had their tea; Will thought the tea had rather a curious taste but Miss Vernon seemed to enjoy it.

Just as they were parting—and parting in a very friendly manner—Will said, "Look here, Miss Vernon, you'll go on holding a watching brief, won't you? I've got to fly home to-night, but I'll be back to fetch them as soon as they can come."

"I'll keep an eye on them," she promised. "And if any other unexpected contingency arises I'll write."

"I'm glad you're here," declared Will, gripping her hand. "I don't see what could happen but you never know."

Chapter 17

Now THAT Will had made up his mind to go home he was so eager to get there that he did not wait to send a cable to his father to say when he was arriving. He caught the first plane and by using various means of transport arrived at Broadmeadows shortly before midnight on the second day.

The house was all shut up but there was still a light in his father's bedroom which meant that his father was awake and reading in bed—or else had dropped off to sleep and omitted to turn it out. Will shouted and threw a handful of gravel at the window, and a few moments later the window was opened from the bottom and Mr. Hastie's head appeared.

" It's me—Will! " cried Will.

" Good heavens, what a time to arrive! " exclaimed Mr. Hastie in justifiable annoyance. " Why didn't you wire or something? I was almost asleep."

" I could climb in by the bathroom window———"

" No, no, wait a moment. I'll come down and let you in."

Will went round to the front door and waited; he had not long to wait. The door was opened by Mr. Hastie clad in a bright red dressing-gown and blue bedroom slippers. His thick white hair was standing on end and his eyes were dazed with sleep.

" If you'd let me know——" he began.

" I'm sorry but I didn't think," explained Will. " All I thought of was getting home as quickly as I could. I've been travelling for two days without stopping and ——"

" Something the matter? " asked Mr. Hastie anxiously.

" Your letter," Will told him. " The moment I got your letter I knew I had to come post-haste. I've found Rae's son."

" What! "

" Rae's son," repeated Will. " I've found him. He's the spit image of Rae. You never saw anything so extra-ordinary, he might be Rae's twin."

" What are you saying? " cried Mr. Hastie in alarm. " Rae wasn't married, so——"

" He was," declared Will. " I found her too—Rae's wife, I mean. I spoke to the old priest who married them."

" You spoke to the old priest . . ."

" Who married them," nodded Will, completing the sentence. " It's absolutely O.K., you can take my word for it, Father."

" Great Scot! " exclaimed Mr. Hastie, and so saying he sat down suddenly upon the chest in the hall, and gazed at Will in astonishment.

" I know," agreed Will. " It's simply staggering isn't it? I was looking for them, of course—at least I was looking for *something*. It was a sort of hunch. I was looking for some sort of mystery—and I found THEM."

" You went over to France on purpose to—to——"

" To nose about," nodded Will. " I didn't say a word

to anybody because it was a sort of wild goose chase—
and then I got a clue and followed it up and asked a lot
of questions—and there they were—as large as life and
twice as natural! "

" You're sure———" began Mr. Hastie.

" Positive. She's the daughter of that Jean Leyrisse
who owned the farm where Rae was billeted. You knew
about Jean Leyrisse, didn't you? "

Mr. Hastie nodded. He was recovering his wits. He
was beginning to believe that this was real, and not a
dream. " What is she like? " he asked in some anxiety.

" Beautiful," said Will simply.

" Beautiful? "

" Charming and delightful—in fact she's a perfect
darling—and the boy is exactly what you would expect
Rae's son to be like. He's a grand little chap, full of
guts and as lively as a cricket."

" I can hardly believe it."

" Oh, I know," agreed Will. " It seems incredible
but it's true. Look here, Father, I must have some food.
I haven't had anything except coffee and biscuits since
breakfast."

" There's half a chicken———"

" Come and watch me eat it and I'll tell you the whole
thing," cried Will joyously.

2

The two Hasties raided the larder and discovered
half a chicken and a piece of boiled ham and several
other odds and ends to allay Will's hunger. Mr. Hastie,
now thoroughly awakened, plied his son with questions

which Will answered as best he could with his mouth full.

" Why on earth didn't Rae tell them about it? " Mr. Hastie wanted to know.

" He was going to, of course, but he wanted to *tell* them—not write. Rae was never much good at writing letters and he was afraid they would worry."

" They would have worried, but still——"

" He was getting leave almost immediately."

" He could have waited——"

" He couldn't have waited," declared Will. " It was in the middle of the war. Things were all queer and hectic; there was no time to think and plan. Nobody knew what was going to happen the next day—or the next hour for that matter."

" Yes, it was like that in the First War," admitted Mr. Hastie.

" Well then, you can understand."

The questions continued. So did Will's meal.

" This'll wipe Master Hugo's eye," said Will with gusto as he cut himself another slice of ham. " I'd like to be there when he hears."

" I wouldn't," declared Mr. Hastie. " Oh, I'm glad the young rotter is to have his eye wiped—as you put it —but I wouldn't care to be present at the wiping. I've read too many wills and it doesn't amuse me to see human beings at their worst . . . and that reminds me we'll have to ca' canny, you know."

" You can ca' as canny as you please."

" It will all have to be cut and dried before we move a step."

" Oh I know," agreed Will, smiling at his father.

" I've found them, but it's over to you now. It's for you to cut and dry . . . but you'll find everything is orlright —as Julie would say."

" Julie? "

" Rae's wife. She speaks English fluently."

" Well, that's a comfort. Does the boy speak English too? "

" As well as I do—better, really. You'll love Tom, he's a most diverting creature."

" Tom? "

" Thomas Rae Elliot Murray."

" Couldn't be better named anyway," said Mr. Hastie approvingly.

Will was silent for a few moments. He remembered Julie saying, " I called him that because we had talked about it—Rae and me. We had talked about having a little son—some day—and Rae said that must be his name. Maman wanted him to be Jean, like my father, and she was cross for a long time, but I could not help it." Remembering this reminded him very vividly of Julie; he wondered what she was doing. Sleeping, of course, thought Will, glancing at the clock. There was the difference in time to consider, which was rather annoying especially as he was not certain whether Nivennes was one hour ahead of Greenwich or two . . . and Summer Time made it even more complicated and confusing.

" What on earth are you thinking about? " asked Mr. Hastie.

" Oh, nothing—really," said Will.

PART THREE

Langford

Chapter 18

PATTY WAS having a very busy time preparing for the arrival of the visitors. She was not excited—that was the strange thing—but examining the reason for her calm she discovered that she did not really believe they were coming. She believed it with her mind—for of course Will would not have told a lie—but she did not believe it in her bones. That was the way Patty explained it to herself. In other words, Patty could not imagine the front door opening and Will walking in with Rae's wife and child.

Mrs. Elliot Murray believed they were coming. She had taken the news quite naturally as if she had known it all along. This seemed queer at first but Patty decided that her mother forgot so many things—and only remembered them when somebody reminded her—that she thought she had known about Julie and Tom. If you walked in a fog (thought Patty), if you groped your way through a cloud—like the cloud on the top of Cloudhill—it would be easy enough to get lost; and if you were lost like that it would be difficult to differentiate between what you knew—and had forgotten—and what you had never known at all.

" It will be lovely to have them," said Mrs. Elliot Murray. " And of course Rae will come as soon as he can. Then we shall all be together again." She added happily, "Will says little Tom is just like Rae so of course he will like all Rae's toys to play with. Don't you think we should get the clockwork train put in order? He's sure to like trains."

"That's a good idea, Margaret," said Colonel Elliot Murray.

Obviously the Colonel had no difficulty in believing that they were coming (perhaps his bones were differently made from Patty's) for it was he who decided that Julie must have the south bedroom, which had a delightful view of the river, and Tom must have his father's room next door.

The rooms were pleasant and convenient but nothing had been done to them for years so the wallpaper was faded and the paint somewhat shabby. Patty pointed this out to her father.

"Yes," agreed the Colonel. "They need redecorating. You had better go and see Logan to-morrow and ask him to do it for us—and get new curtains and covers for the chairs while you're about it. Get it done at once."

It had been decided, on the advice of Mr. Hastie, to keep the news a secret until everything was " cut and dried," but in a small place like Torfoot nothing remains a secret. Rumours had spread like wild-fire—so when Patty visited the local painter and decorator prepared to plead with him on bended knee for the work to be put in hand without delay she found him unexpectedly co-operative.

"Yes, of course," said Mr. Logan. " I thought you'd be wanting some painting done. If you'd like to choose a paper this morning we could get started right away. Have you any idea when the visitors will be coming, Miss Patty? "

" Well—no—not exactly," replied Patty uncomfortably.

" I better put three men on the job," said Mr. Logan.

Mr. Logan was so nice that Patty wished she could tell him all about it—and it seemed rather silly not to, for obviously he knew the whole story already—but Mr. Hastie had said they were not to mention it to anybody at all. (" Of course there will be rumours," Mr. Hastie had said. " We all know Torfoot, but as long as none of the family mentions the subject no action can be taken.")

Mr. Logan was discreet; he asked no questions about the mysterious visitors; but when Patty had chosen the wallpapers and emerged from the shop she found herself face to face with Mrs. Hunter Brown . . . and it was obvious that Mrs. Hunter Brown had been lying in wait for her.

" What's this I hear? " inquired the redoubtable lady. " Is it true, Patty? It sounds a most extraordinary tale."

" Oh! " exclaimed Patty. " Oh—well—I don't know what you've heard——"

" You know perfectly well," declared Mrs. Hunter Brown. " The whole town is steaming with the news that Rae was secretly married and his wife is coming to Langford."

" I c-can't tell you—definitely. We d-don't know for certain ourselves," stammered Patty . . . and she turned and fled.

It was ignominious—and impolite—but what else

could she do? Patty was aware that she was no match for Mrs. Hunter Brown.

After that unfortunate encounter Patty took care to do her shopping very early in the morning when there was less chance of meeting any of her neighbours.

Will had mentioned the " quiet pony " which he had promised Tom, so Colonel Elliot Murray put advertisements in some of the local papers and received several replies. Amongst them was a letter from Colonel Roger Ayrton of Amberwell. He explained that he had a very quiet pony which was now too small for his son and he was willing to dispose of it.

" That sounds hopeful," said Will when he was shown the letter. " I know Ayrton quite well—we soldiered together in Africa—he's an awfully decent fellow. I could go over and have a look at it."

" I'll go myself," said the Colonel.

" Go over to Westkirk! " cried Patty. " You can't possibly. It would be far too tiring for you, Daddy."

" I don't think so———"

" It would—really," declared Patty, taking a firm line. " Will and I can go and see the pony. We'll take a picnic lunch and make a day of it. Let's ring up Colonel Ayrton and ask if we can see the pony to-morrow afternoon."

" Oh, very well, Patty," said her father meekly.

2

Patty had not been to Westkirk before and had not realised that it was near the sea, so she was pleasantly surprised when they rounded a bend in the road and saw the little town and the sea beyond, stretching blue and calm to the far horizon.

" How lovely! " she exclaimed impulsively.

" Yes, it's a charming place," agreed Will. " I haven't been here since I was a boy and I'd forgotten how nice it was . . . but I remember it now. Shall we go down to the harbour? "

" Yes, let's," said Patty. " There's no hurry. We could have our lunch on the shore, couldn't we? "

The tide was in and the harbour was full of little boats bobbing up and down on the gentle swell. They were mostly fishing-boats which had been out early and had returned with their catch. There were fishermen sorting out the gleaming fish and packing them into boxes for the market, and there were old men and young girls sitting upon the jetty mending nets. It was a peaceful scene and for a while Patty and Will watched it with interest and pleasure. Then, leaving the car, they walked along the edge of the sea. The sun was golden, the air was sparklingly clear and there was a faint westerly breeze with the scent of the sea in it. Presently they discovered a little bay, sheltered by rocks. There was a tiny cave in the cliff with a sandy floor. It was an ideal place for their picnic.

" A smugglers' cave! " exclaimed Patty in delight.

" Well, perhaps," said Will, smiling. " It's a bit too small really, but we can pretend it's a smugglers' cave, can't we? "

" It's a heavenly place, anyway."

Will could not deny that. " Quite perfect," he agreed. " And the odd thing is I appreciate it all the more after my trip to France. The sun was so hot in Nivennes;

it was simply baking. You couldn't sit in the sunshine like this—or at least I couldn't. Julie enjoyed it, of course."

" Tell me more about Julie. Do you think she'll be happy at Langford? Somehow I can't believe she's real."

" She's real, all right . . . but I know what you mean, Patty."

Patty waited. She had asked him to tell her " more about Julie" but he was silent. He was gazing into the distance where the Isle of Arran rose from the sea—the mountains seemed to be floating in the crystal clear air. For the first time Patty realised that Will had not talked very much about Julie; he had told them a lot about Tom, but beyond saying that she was "beautiful" and he was sure they would like her he had scarcely mentioned her name. Patty might have repeated her request but she did not like to, for since his return from France there was a slight constraint between them. Even to-day, although they had chatted and laughed, they were not absolutely comfortable together as they had been before.

Behind where they were sitting there was a stony path which mounted steeply between bushes and vanished in a green tunnel of wind-blown trees.

" I wonder where it goes," said Patty thoughtfully. " There's something rather fascinating about it, isn't there? "

" No time to explore," replied Will. " It's time to get on with our job. We've got to find Amberwell and see the pony—and all that."

" Yes, I suppose so," agreed Patty.

Actually they were sitting upon Amberwell property and if they had climbed the path it would have led them through the gardens to the house, but they were not to know this, of course, so they finished their meal and, rising reluctantly, walked back to the harbour.

Chapter 19

THERE WAS no difficulty in finding Amberwell. The first
man they asked told them it was the big gates just
beyond St. Stephen's Church and they could not miss it
. . . and although Will had been given these sort of
directions on other occasions and had missed his objective
quite easily he realised that on this occasion the statement
was correct. Nobody could have missed seeing the gates
of Amberwell unless they had been blind.

The gates stood open and as they turned in a boy of
about fourteen or fifteen years old rose from a stone
where he had been sitting and signalled to them to
stop. With him was a girl, slightly smaller than himself
—a fairy-like creature with silky brown hair and wide
grey eyes.

" Have you come to see Dapple? " asked the boy.

" Yes," said Will, smiling.

" Then I suppose you're Colonel Elliot Murray? "

Will explained the circumstances.

" Oh well—that's all right," said the boy, nodding.
" Dad had to go out but he'll be back soon. He said I
was to take you down to the paddock. I'm Stephen
Ayrton and this is Emmie."

" The pony belongs to you? "

Stephen nodded.

"Stephen is too big for him now," explained Emmie. "And of course it's frightfully dull for Dapple when we're both away at school. He likes a lot of petting."

"We'll go and look at him, shall we?" Will suggested.

The two got into the car and they drove on up the avenue. Everything was well-kept; it was a beautiful place with trees and flowers and bushes in perfect order. Patty noticed rare plants which she had never seen before and others which she had seen growing in greenhouses.

"It must be warm here!" she exclaimed in surprise.

"It's the Gulf Stream," said Emmie. "And of course Amberwell is very sheltered. There are several palm-trees, you know. Lots of people come to look at them and admire them."

"Pretend to admire them," said Stephen scornfully. "Nobody could really admire them because they're ugly. I like things growing in their proper place. Palms may be all right in the desert but they look silly here—and they aren't nearly so nice as chestnut trees or beeches. At least that's what I think."

Patty was inclined to agree.

By this time they had reached the house, a well-designed building of grey stone. It was not as large as Langford, nor as beautiful, but it looked solid and comfortable.

"That's Amberwell," said Stephen—somewhat unnecessarily—but this time there was pride, not scorn, in his voice. He added, "I don't know whether you're interested in houses but it was built by my great-great-great-great-grandfather in 1805—and there have been Ayrtons here ever since."

" You've missed out a great," said Emmie.

" No I haven't! "

" Yes you have. There ought to be five greats. Old William was mine too."

" Shall I park the car here? " asked Will, cutting short the argument.

They left the car standing in the drive and walked down to the paddock, a sheltered meadow with several shady trees. The pony was grazing contentedly but came at once when Stephen called his name. He was dapple-grey—which was only to be expected—with a soft brown nose and a long grey tail. Patty was enchanted with him and was about to say so when she caught Will's eye and saw him shake his head. For a moment she was under the impression that for some reason the pony would not do, and then she realised that she was being warned to disguise her enthusiasm. Meanwhile Will was examining the pony thoroughly, looking at the creature's teeth and eyes, lifting each hoof in turn and running a firm hand down his legs. Then Dapple was saddled and bridled and Emmie mounted and rode him round the field.

All this time Stephen had leant upon the gate beside Patty and watched in silence.

" You won't want to part with him," said Patty at last.

" No, I've been miserable about it," Stephen replied. " You see, I've had him so long—and he really is nice. You think he's nice, don't you, Miss Elliot Murray? "

" He's a darling," Patty declared. " He's an absolute pet. You needn't worry, Stephen. We shall all love Dapple."

" I'm not worrying so much. Major Hastie knows all about ponies—you can see that—and Dapple likes him. Dapple lets me do anything to him but he doesn't like strangers looking at his mouth—not even the vet."

" He didn't mind Major Hastie——"

" That's what I mean," nodded Stephen.

Patty had forgotten that she was to disguise her enthusiasm; she only thought of comforting Stephen for the loss of his pet, and of reassuring Stephen's mind about Dapple's future. She explained that the pony was to be a surprise for her nephew who had been brought up in France and was coming home to Langford . . . oddly enough she found herself telling Stephen quite a lot about Tom. In return she learned that Stephen's mother had been killed in the war (just like Tom's father) when Stephen was a baby, and she learned that Stephen had a step-mother of whom he was very fond.

" She's awfully decent," declared Stephen. " You'll see her when we go back to the house."

There was no time to say more. Emmie trotted the pony up to the gate and Patty stroked him and told him he was beautiful—though it was obvious he knew this already—then he was unsaddled and turned loose and the four human beings left him to graze in peace.

2

When Colonel Ayrton returned he was surprised to see Will Hastie—whom he knew—instead of the stranger with whom he had corresponded. The two greeted each other cordially and immediately began to talk of experiences they had shared in the North African campaign. The pony was not mentioned, but Patty supposed they would remember about it presently.

" Would you like to see my sisters, Miss Elliot Murray? " suggested Stephen.

" You had better say yes," said Emmie with a mischievous chuckle. " Stephen is terribly proud of his sisters."

" I'm not! " exclaimed Stephen. " I just thought she might like to see them. I mean most ladies like seeing them—and it's no use hanging about. Those two will go on talking for hours. We might just as well leave them to it and have a look at Isabel and Elinor."

Patty had supposed that Emmie was Stephen's sister—and said so.

" Oh no, I'm only Stephen's cousin," Emmie explained. " We've got thousands of cousins, of course. Some of them are nice but others are rather poor value——"

" Why bother Miss Elliot Murray with all that? " muttered Stephen.

" I thought she might be interested. Perhaps she's got thousands of cousins herself."

Patty disclaimed this. " Only one," she said. She hesitated, but they were both looking at her so she added, " I thought he was nice—but—but I've changed my mind about him."

" Poor value," said Emmie, nodding understandingly.

" Come on," said Stephen, changing the subject. " Let's go and look at Isabel and Elinor."

Patty followed the two round the corner of the house and found herself upon a terrace with a stone balustrade.

At one end of the terrace stood an unusually large pram with a canopy over it, and in the pram lay two large babies. They were alike as two peas, with chubby faces and curly brown hair, and both were lost in profound slumber. Their fat little hands were relaxed peacefully and their long dark eyelashes lay softly upon their rose-petal cheeks in the prettiest way imaginable.

" Oh, how beautiful! " exclaimed Patty involuntarily.

" They're only my half-sisters of course," said Stephen with a casual air which did not deceive his companions.

" Two halves make a whole," suggested Emmie.

" That's not a bad joke," he admitted. " I'll remember that. Two halves make a whole."

Meanwhile Patty had been gazing at the babies in admiration. " Can you tell them apart? " she inquired.

" Good lord, yes," replied Stephen. " That's Isabel and that's Elinor. They aren't a bit alike when you know them. Isabel is much better value."

At this moment Isabel opened her eyes. She yawned like a little cat and then sat up and looked round at her admirers.

" Gosh! " exclaimed Emmie in alarm. " We've wakened her. Nannie will be hopping mad! "

" Stee! " said Isabel, holding out her arms.

" She knows me, you see," said Stephen. He went forward and, picking her up, shook her in the air. " Bundle of rubbish, aren't you? " he added fondly.

" Stee! " gurgled Isabel ecstatically.

" Wait till Nannie sees you! " exclaimed Emmie.

Patty did not know very much about babies but even she was aware that Stephen's behaviour was unorthodox,

so she was fully prepared for trouble when the twins'
lawful guardian suddenly appeared upon the scene.
Nannie was a little old woman in a large white apron.
Her wrinkled face was screwed up into a savage frown.

"Stephen! How often have I told you——" cried
Nannie.

"Hundreds of times," admitted Stephen cheerfully.
"But you know quite well I can't resist Isabel when
she calls me Stee, so it isn't the least use being cross
with me."

"I'm very cross."

"You're not really, Nannie. You're trying not to
smile. Look here, I'll carry them up to the nursery.
They get heavier and heavier every day," added Stephen,
and so saying he caught up a half-sister under each arm
as if they had been two bundles of washing and marched
off. All that was visible of the babies was two round
bottoms in bright blue knickers and four fat bare legs
waving wildly in the air.

"Did you ever see the like!" cried Nannie, hastening
after them.

"They're going to have their tea," explained Emmie.
"It's an awfully amusing show, so if you don't mind
——" and with that she joined the procession.

3

Abandoned by her companions Patty leant upon the
balustrade and laughed immoderately . . . but presently
she recovered her composure and wondered what to do.
It seemed odd to remain here alone, but it seemed even
odder to prowl round a strange house looking for an

unknown hostess. Fortunately she was rescued from her predicament quite soon. Mrs. Ayrton came hurrying out of the house and explained with profuse apologies that she had no idea Miss Elliot Murray had come.

"Men are so funny," said Mrs. Ayrton. "When they get together and talk about their reminiscences they forget everything else. It wasn't until Roger said you would be here for tea that I realised we had another guest. You *must* have thought it queer."

There was no doubt about the identity of Mrs. Ayrton; she was extremely like her daughters. She was not so beautiful of course (it is doubtful whether any grown-up person could have been as beautiful as the twins) but she was charming and attractive with a round rosy face and dark curls.

"It's very kind of you to ask us to tea but I don't think we can stay," said Patty doubtfully.

"I'm afraid you'll have to," Mrs. Ayrton replied. "Honestly I don't think you'll be able to tear Major Hastie out of Roger's clutches—and tea is ready in the morning-room so we may as well have it."

The invitation did not sound gracious but Patty understood exactly what was meant. Mrs. Ayrton's amendment was unnecessary.

"Of course it's lovely for me to have you," added Mrs. Ayrton hastily. "I just meant that if they're expecting you home—but you could ring up, couldn't you?"

"Perhaps I'd better," agreed Patty, and she explained that her father was the sort of person who worried inordinately if people were late.

When they had rung up Langford Mrs. Ayrton led

the way to the morning-room where tea was laid out upon a round table near the french window, and Patty, on beholding the welcome sight, could not help wondering whether her hostess possessed a well-trained staff or had spread the feast with her own fair hands (a natural reaction nowadays as everybody is bound to admit). Patty did not mention this, of course, for as yet she did not know her hostess well enough to inquire into her domestic arrangements. Instead she murmured politely, " What a delightful room! "

" I'm glad you like it," returned Mrs. Ayrton. " I've always thought it the nicest room in the house. It gets all the morning sunshine and it's so much smaller and cosier than the drawing-room. We always use this room when we can. Of course when the family comes we can't." She plugged in the electric kettle and added, " Roger likes to keep open house for all his relations—he has three sisters, with families, and a brother in the Navy —so sometimes Amberwell is like a hotel. As a matter of fact Roger and I are away ourselves a good deal. He's still in the Army, you know."

" He doesn't want to retire? " asked Patty. She added, " I mean, Amberwell is such a lovely place."

" Roger won't retire if I can help it," said his wife firmly. " Roger is a soldier through and through, and there wouldn't be nearly enough for him to do at Amber-well to keep him happy. He would be bored stiff in six months. Sometimes I wish we could retire—I love this place and I have two babies. Usually we cart the babies along," said Mrs. Ayrton, smiling, " but sometimes it isn't possible and I have to leave them at home."

"With Nannie," suggested Patty, returning the smile.

"Oh, you've seen Nannie, have you?"

Patty replied that she had; she also gave an account of her introduction to Isabel and Elinor.

"Dear Stephen!" exclaimed Mrs. Ayrton. "He's devoted to the babies! I was so afraid he might resent them but he's been quite perfect about it. Of course it was lovely when the babies arrived—we were in Singapore at the time—but I couldn't help worrying about Stephen. You see, I've known Stephen since he was a baby, his mother was my greatest friend . . ."

Thus chatting in a friendly manner, Mrs. Ayrton made tea and very soon the two warriors came in to share it.

4

Mrs. Ayrton's prophecy proved correct and it was late when Will and Patty took the road home. The two warriors had re-fought several battles and had agreed to meet again at an early date to re-fight more. Last but not least, Dapple's future had been decided in a manner satisfactory to all concerned.

"He's just the pony for Tom," declared Will as they swept out of Amberwell gates and breasted the hill. "Ayrton wants a good price for him, but he's worth it . . . and we can have him on approval so your father can see him; as a matter of fact I'm sure your father will buy him for Tom."

Patty was sure of it too.

"The Ayrtons are nice, aren't they?" said Will.

"It's fun meeting people like Roger Ayrton—people you can talk to about things that happened in the war and all that. I hope you weren't bored."

"No, of course not. Mrs. Ayrton is a dear; we got on awfully well. If you're asking them to come over to Broadmeadows you can ask me too."

"Good plan! We'll ask them to lunch."

"Do you ever wish you were still in the Service?"

"Not really—perhaps just once or twice when I was feeling a bit fed up—but Ayrton and I are quite different. He's all set for promotion so it would be silly for him to retire. His wife likes Army life," explained Will.

Patty said nothing and after a few moments' silence Will added, "When you see people like that, so happy together, it makes you think."

"You mean think about getting married?"

"Well—perhaps——"

Glancing at him sideways, Patty saw that he was smiling in a vague sort of way. She was surprised. Somehow she had never thought of Will getting married. It seemed a most extraordinary idea—and yet why should it seem extraordinary? Now that Patty thought about it seriously she realised that Will's life at Broadmeadows must be rather dull and lonely. Mr. Hastie was a dear, but all the same . . . Patty wondered if Will had anyone in mind or whether he was just thinking of marriage in general terms after seeing the domestic felicity of the Ayrtons. She decided upon the latter alternative for, having reviewed all the marriageable females in the district, she could think of nobody good enough for Will.

Chapter 20

Colonel Elliot Murray was delighted when he heard that the expedition to Westkirk had been so successful, and was even more delighted when the pony arrived in a trailer and was led out on to the gravel sweep in front of Langford House. Will was there, of course. He had made a point of being present, for he was anxious to see whether the Colonel approved of his choice. Fortunately all was well. Indeed the Colonel was so interested in the pony that he himself made all the arrangements for its welfare.

The paddock needed new fencing (like many other things at Langford nobody had bothered about it for years) and until this was done the pony was bedded with peat in a loose-box, and old MacLaggan's grandson, who "had a way with beasts," was engaged to look after the little creature and to exercise it daily. Young Mac-Laggan took his duties seriously and enjoyed them, but all the same Colonel Elliot Murray was in and out of the stable constantly to see that all was well with his new acquisition and could often be found leaning upon the gate of the paddock watching it being exercised.

In a way Patty was glad of this, but she was a little anxious as to whether all this walking and standing about was good for an elderly gentleman who had spent most of the summer sitting in a chair. She pursued him whenever she could and begged him not to tire himself unduly.

" I don't seem to feel tired," replied her father. " It's the weather, I expect. There's a nice nip in the air. Hot weather doesn't suit me—you know that, Patty. He's a pretty creature, isn't he? We were lucky to get him. I hope Tom will like him."

Patty thought that Tom would be hard to please if he did not like his pony.

Mr. Hastie, who had heard all this and a great deal more from Will, was worried too but on a different score. He went over to Langford and found his old friend walking about in the paddock watching the pony being exercised.

" Look here, Thomas," he said. " Have you got in touch with your lawyers? You want to be perfectly certain——"

" I wrote to Arbuthnot yesterday—told him to make inquiries and let me know—but it will be all right, I'm sure. What do you think of the pony? He's a nice little beast, isn't he? There isn't a grain of vice in him— you can see that—and of course he's used to children. He's really just a children's pet."

Mr. Hastie agreed that he was just the right sort of pony for a boy to start on—he was not unlike the rocking-horse which had been the joy of Will's heart when Will was six years old.

" He's called Dapple, isn't he? " said Mr. Hastie.

" Yes, that's what the Ayrtons called him," replied the Colonel, smiling. " But it seems to me a bit too obvious so I've decided to call him Scottie instead."

Mr. Hastie was not really very interested in the pony's name. He said, " But look here, Thomas, I told you we ought to be careful. We ought to keep the whole thing a dead secret until everything has been cut and dried."

" I haven't said anything."

" Perhaps not, but you're having rooms prepared and you've bought a pony. Everybody in Torfoot knows the whole story. Hugo is bound to hear about it before long."

" What does it matter? "

" It matters a lot. There'll be real trouble when Hugo hears."

" Hugo can do nothing," said the Colonel cheerfully. " Arbuthnot will write to him and tell him—and that will be that. Neither Hugo nor anybody else can prevent Rae's son from inheriting Langford."

This was true, of course, but all the same Mr. Hastie was worried . . . which was all the more strange because Mr. Hastie was not given to worrying, and Colonel Elliot Murray *was*.

By this time it was late September and the trees had put on their autumn tints of golden and red and copper. All round Langford they stood like flaming torches. There were flames in the grass too, where some of their leaves had fallen. Gladioli and chrysanthemums were blooming in the garden, the heather had faded and the hills were tawny like a lion's hide.

The coming of Julie and Tom had been put off several times on account of Madame Leyrisse, who continued to have queer turns of giddiness whenever a date was suggested, and although the doctor could find nothing

wrong it was impossible for Julie to leave her . . . but
at last Miss Vernon wrote to say that she had taken it
upon herself to engage an exceedingly capable woman
to look after Madame Leyrisse in her daughter's absence,
and Major Hastie had better come over immediately.
She was sorry to be so sudden but if the opportunity
were missed it was doubtful whether Julie and Tom
would ever be able to get away at all. They would come
for three weeks, said Miss Vernon. Three weeks was
not long but it was better than nothing. They could
meet and talk things over and make plans.

Will flew over the next day and a week later the
Colonel received a cable with the news that they would
all arrive at Langford on Tuesday evening.

2

Patty had been unable to imagine the front door opening and Will walking in with Rae's wife and child, but
that is what happened—or at least it was so nearly what
happened as to make no odds. She was putting the final
touches to their rooms when she heard the car and
rushed down like a whirlwind. The front door opened
and Will walked in with a woman clinging to his arm.
Patty had thought of her sister-in-law a great deal and
had wondered what she would be like. She had expected
to see somebody very smart and chic, poised and self-
assured, somebody resembling Yvonne Arnaud in her
younger days (Yvonne Arnaud was Patty's idea of what
a Frenchwoman should look like); but this woman bore
no resemblance to Yvonne Arnaud. She looked frightened
and pathetic; she was swathed in woollen scarves and

her small round face peeped out of the wrappings like a scared mouse.

Patty had been scared herself, but now all she wanted was to reassure her visitor so it was easy to put her arms round Julie's shoulders and to exclaim, " Oh, you must be tired! Such a long journey! "

" But no, I am not tired," said Julie in a very small voice. " Will took such care of us that it was no bother. It is nice of you to be so kind."

" Patty will look after you," said Will. " I must fetch Tom. He's asleep in the back of the car, so I'll carry him in and we can put him straight to bed."

" I've wakened up now," said Tom. He had come up the steps and was standing in the open doorway beneath the light. His hair was ruffled, so that the tuft on the top of his head stood straight on end, and his wide blue eyes were dazed.

It's Rae! thought Patty. She had been prepared to see a little boy who looked like Rae but this resemblance was startling. There was something a little uncanny about it. She could not speak.

" Where's the Colonel? " asked Will. " He'll want to see them, won't he? I'll bring in the luggage."

" But I must take off my things! " cried Julie. " I must brush Tom's hair and wash his hands before his grand-father sees him! " She was peeling off her scarves as she spoke and heaping them on to a chair.

It was at this moment that Mrs. Elliot Murray came out of the morning-room, followed by the Colonel.

" Here we are," said Will. " I'm afraid we're a bit late but we couldn't help it."

The Colonel hesitated, gazing at his grandson almost

incredulously, but Mrs. Elliot Murray ran forward and took the boy in her arms.

" Oh, you are just like Rae! " she cried joyfully. " You are just like my own darling Rae! " Then she turned to Julie. " And we shall all love you dearly—because Rae loves you."

" And a little for myself too, I hope," said Julie as she accepted and returned the warm embrace.

Meanwhile Tom had gone forward to meet his grandfather. " I've come to see you," said Tom.

" I'm very glad," declared the Colonel. He had put his hand on Tom's head and was smoothing down his hair.

" We came in an aeroplane," said Tom. " I had never been in one before but I liked it—and I wasn't sick." He took a deep breath and added, " Grandfather, do you think I could have a pony? "

" Oh, Tom! " exclaimed Julie in dismay. " You must not ask——"

Neither of them heard.

" There's a pony in the stable," said the Colonel, smiling down at the vivid, eager face. " He's there, waiting for you, Tom. You shall see him to-morrow morning."

" Oh! " cried Tom, flushing to the roots of his unruly hair. " Oh, I can hardly believe it! Oh, not a pony of my own? "

The Colonel nodded. " Of your very own," he said.

" I suppose I couldn't see him now, could I? " asked Tom. " It's late, of course—and he might be asleep— but perhaps if I went in very quietly."

The Colonel laughed and took up an electric torch

which lay upon the hall table. He held out his hand to Tom and the two went down the steps together and disappeared into the darkness.

" Oh dear! " exclaimed Julie. " Is that orlright? "

" It's—wonderfully right," declared Patty with a sigh of relief.

" He never said anything to Julie! " cried Mrs. Elliot Murray in dismay. " How queer of Thomas not to——"

" He did not see me," said Julie quickly. " He saw only Tom. It does not matter at all."

" Come upstairs, Julie," said Patty. " You'll want to see your room. We'll have supper in about twenty minutes; by that time Tom will have seen the pony and be ready for some food."

Julie was delighted with her room—she would have been hard to please if she had not been delighted—" How spacious! " she exclaimed. " How pretty, and fresh! Oh, it is kind to make so much preparation for us! And Tom is next door! Oh, it could not be nicer! Will told me about Langford but I did not think it would be so big and grand."

" It isn't really big and grand," said Patty, smiling.

" It is to me," declared Julie. " Villa des Cygnes is very small in deed . . ."

Julie had sat down before the dressing-table and was brushing her hair and coiling it deftly into the knot which she wore at the nape of her neck. Will had said she was " beautiful " but Patty did not see it. She was attractive and charming — her skin was so smooth and her hair so glossy—and her manners were very sweet.

" Will told me a lot about you," said Julie, who had

been "taking stock" also. "He said you were like a sister to him. Is that right?"

Patty nodded. "Absolutely right. Rae and Will and I grew up together. It was just like having two brothers —and when Will came back to live at Broadmeadows he was just the same."

"He is like a brother still?"

"Yes, of course."

"That is what I wanted to know," explained Julie.

At the time this little conversation seemed quite unimportant. It was interrupted by Tom, who came in full of excitement at having seen his pony—seen him awake and eager to be petted! He was beautiful—oh so beautiful! He was the most beautiful pony in the world. Tom had stroked Scottie's soft nose and given him an apple! His grandfather had shown him the proper way to do it.

"That is very nice," said Julie. "I hope you thanked your grandfather very nicely."

"No!" exclaimed Tom in dismay. "No, I forgot! I never said thank you at all."

They both looked so horrified at this lapse of memory that Patty burst out laughing.

"Oh, how can you laugh!" exclaimed Julie. "It is dreadful. It is so ungrateful and naughty when his grandfather is so kind."

"His grandfather saw his face. Tom's face said thank you better than words. Honestly, Julie, there's no need to worry . . ."

But Julie was not listening. She was talking to her son in a rapid flow of French; telling him he must wash his face and hands and comb his hair and he must run downstairs very quickly and say thank you for the so generous gift, and he must explain that he had forgotten to say it before because he had been " bouleversé " by the beauty of the little horse . . . and so on . . . and so on . . . and Tom agreed that he must go at once and repair the omission and perhaps he could give his so kind grandfather a little kiss—un tout petit baiser—or would that not be the correct thing for a boy who was half English to do?

They are darlings, thought Patty (who spoke French none too badly and could understand every word). They really are perfectly sweet—and she joined in the conversation by giving it as her considered opinion that under the circumstances " un tout petit baiser " would not be out of place.

" À la bonne heure! " cried Julie rapturously. "You speak French—and how well! We will speak French together sometimes, n'est-ce pas, chère Patty? "

Chapter 21

LIFE AT Langford had run in a groove for years and Patty
had wondered how the parents would react to the changed
conditions. She soon discovered that the change suited
everybody in the household—everybody was more
cheerful. The old house seemed to stir and come alive.
Was it too fanciful to think that the old house was
pleased at the sound of a child's voice within its walls?
The house, which had seemed empty, was empty no
longer. The queer feeling of incompleteness had
vanished . . . for although Tom was a quiet little boy
and his mother kept him in order his presence pervaded
the whole place. In a very few days Tom had dug himself in. He rode Scottie in the morning and walked with
his grandfather in the afternoon. These two were
already good companions. They had started well and
they continued even better. Patty was surprised at the
way they chatted together, for although she and Rae
had loved their father dearly they had never found very
much to say to him.

Patty had expected to be busy—there was always
so much to do when people came to stay—but she found
she was less busy than usual.

"You will give me little duties," Julie said. " I will
be happier if I have things to do. I will keep our rooms

—that, of course—but it will not be enough. At home there was much to do."

The old custom of "tea in the play-room" was revived and one wet afternoon Patty produced the clockwork train and showed Tom how to fix the rails together—and presently the trains ran round the floor in and out of the furniture with the familiar chattering noise and Tom went after them on his hands and knees winding them up.

It was that afternoon, when they were having tea, that the Colonel appeared at the door. He had not climbed the steep wooden stairs for years—even in the old days he had never gone up to the play-room. The play-room had always been "for the children," it had been quite apart from the rest of the house . . . but here was the Colonel, smiling and asking if there were a cup of tea for him, and sitting down in the old basket-chair where Rae had so often sat.

" This place needs doing up," he declared as he looked at the well-worn surroundings. " I had no idea it had got so shabby. You need a new carpet for one thing and that blind is a perfect disgrace. You had better see to it, Patty."

" I like it," said Patty hastily. " we all like it. Honestly Daddy, we don't want anything changed——"

" The blind is quite rotten. It must have been hanging there for years."

" That's why we like it," said Patty simply.

The following day was Saturday, which was Patty's shopping morning, and Julie asked leave to accompany her to Torfoot.

" I do all the marketing for my mother," Julie

explained. " So I shall be very interested to see the way you do it."

Patty was delighted, of course; they set out together very happily and, leaving the car in the car-park, walked down the main street.

Everybody in the place knew Patty and everybody had heard about the new arrivals, so they were stopped a dozen times in as many yards by people who wanted a chat.

" It will be frightfully difficult for you, Julie," said Patty when she had introduced her sister-in-law to at least seven different people. " Everybody will remember you——"

" And I shall not remember them," agreed Julie with a sigh. " I shall try very hard, of course, and perhaps if I smile at everyone it will not cause offence." She added in a puzzled voice, " But this is a funny way to do your marketing. There is one butcher only, and you do not bargain with him. You do not ask the price—nor pay him! "

" We pay at the end of the month," explained Patty. " It's easier."

" It is a little dull, I think. Perhaps we are greedy but food is very important to us. We go to the market and——"

" Yes, but we haven't got a market and Mr. Fraser would think I'd gone mad if I tried to bargain with him over the price of chops. It's different here, that's all."

" I am surprised continually," declared Julie. " I am surprised at some things because they are different and at other things because they are the same. You see, Patty, if you walked with me in Nivennes all the people would know about you and want to meet you. They would be so pleased to see you and they would ask if you had a good journey and if you were tired and if you liked Nivennes and they would say you spoke French very nicely—and it was so clever of you—and they would remember you afterwards and be a little bit cross if you did not remember them. All that would be the same. But to have only one butcher and one baker and one shop for buying vegetables—and you do not ask the price! "

" This is my sister-in-law," said Patty. She had said the same words over and over again. They were silly words really, because everybody knew already that Julie was her sister-in-law, but what else could she say?

This time it was to Mrs. Hunter Brown of Mosslands who had just emerged from her ancient Humber and was advancing upon them with a welcoming smile.

" Oh, how nice to see you! " exclaimed Mrs. Hunter Brown. " We heard you were coming to Langford. Did you have a good journey? I expect you were very tired. How do you like Torfoot? "

Patty was giggling feebly, pretending to blow her nose, but Julie was made of sterner stuff and was answering very prettily; saying she had had a very nice journey thank you, and she was not tired at all, and Torfoot was a very nice place.

" You speak English beautifully—so clever of you! " said Mrs. Hunter Brown approvingly. " Patty must bring you over to lunch."

2

Julie was a delightful companion for Patty. They had fun together and they talked—sometimes in English and sometimes in French. They went to lunch at Mosslands and to tea at Peacehaven. They walked through the woods or over the moors. Sometimes Tom went with them, riding Scottie.

Julie had brought with her from Nivennes a box of herbs—they looked like tiny white flowers—and from these she made an infusion with boiling water. She drank a cup of this curious brew at night when she went to bed.

" It helps one to sleep," she explained to Patty.

" Aren't you sleeping well?" asked Patty anxiously.

" Not very well," replied Julie. " Oh, I am very comfortable. I have everything—no, there is nothing I want—but *nothing!* "

" Then why——"

" It is just that I feel a little bit strange. I mean things are different from Nivennes. Perhaps in a little while I shall get used to it and I shall sleep better. Then there will be no need for tisane."

Patty was not sleeping well either so one night she accepted a cup of tisane. Perhaps it helped a little— and the flavour was not unpleasant.

After that it became a habit. Patty went along to Julie's room in her dressing-gown and sat on Julie's bed and they drank tisane together—and chatted. The habit cemented their friendship for when two young women get together in their dressing-gowns they can talk to each other about matters which are close to their hearts.

It was odd that Patty was not sleeping well for usually she was a champion sleeper. Usually Patty got into bed and put her head on her pillow and slept like a top until the morning . . . but for some reason this pleasant aptitude for slumber had left her. Everything was going splendidly—nothing could have been better—and yet Patty was not entirely happy. She was like the princess in the fairy-tale who could not rest comfortably and did not know the cause of her unease. The cause was a dried pea and although it was hidden beneath twelve thicknesses of mattress it troubled the princess and interfered with her sleep.

I ought to be happy, Patty told herself. There's absolutely nothing to worry about. Daddy has got what he wanted: a grandson to inherit Langford. Mummy is not nearly so lost and miserable; Tom is settling down better than anybody could possibly have expected and Julie is a dear. Why am I not happy? What on earth is the matter with me?

And then, suddenly, she knew.

3

Will had not been to Langford since the night he had brought Julie and Tom. He had telephoned twice to ask how things were going and was delighted to hear such excellent reports. He explained that having been away from home for over a week he was exceedingly busy . . . and he was further "tied up" with a specialist in Work Study who was staying at Broadmeadows and making notes about the condition of the farms on the estate and giving their owners useful advice upon modern methods and equipment.

" Come soon," said Patty.

" As soon as ever I can," declared Will.

At last Will managed to escape and appeared unexpectedly one afternoon at tea-time. Julie and Patty and Tom were having tea in the play-room and Will was welcomed with open arms.

Tom was especially vociferous in his welcome (he and Will were old friends) and he had so much to say about all he had been doing that it was difficult for anybody else to get a word in. Usually when Tom talked too much he was curbed gently by his mother but to-day she gave him rein.

Presently however Tom paused for breath, there was a lull in the chatter and Patty had her chance.

" Oh, Will," she began, " I wanted to ask you——"

But Will was not listening. Will was looking at Julie —and Julie was looking at Will.

The silence lasted a few moments. That was all.

" Will! " cried Tom. " Will, you've finished your tea, haven't you? Come and see Scottie. We'll take an apple for him; you can give him half of it if you like. Will, listen! Come and see Scottie *now*! "

Will laughed and they went off together to the stables. Julie followed them but Patty remained in the play-room. She sat down in the big basket-chair near the window and tried to sort things out.

Now that she knew—or guessed—everything fitted together and made sense. For instance Julie had said that they would come to Langford for three weeks to talk things over and make plans, but time was running on and there had been no talk of the future, no plans had been made. Patty had wondered about that. She had wondered anxiously what her father would do when they went away. She had wondered what plans were in Julie's mind about the future. She could have asked of course but it had seemed better not to ask. Indeed she had been afraid to broach the subject. She was sure that her father shared her fears. He too was afraid that Julie and Tom would return to Nivennes and remain there indefinitely—coming over to Langford for an occasional visit but not making it their home.

All this time there had been a feeling that " something was going to happen " and now Patty knew what it was. Of course it was much the best solution to the problem; Julie would go to Broadmeadows and Tom would stay at Langford. It was the perfect solution. Patty ought to have been delighted but she was not.

I'm crazy, said Patty to herself. Will has always been my friend; he has always been my brother—or almost —so what more do I want? But Will was not really her brother and the fact remained that when she had seen Will and Julie look at each other "like that" it had given her a strange pain in her heart. He's the same but I've changed, thought Patty. Well, I'll just have to bear it.

She would have to bear it—and perhaps it would not last. Perhaps some day the pain would go away and she would be able to feel happy about Will and Julie. It was her own fault of course. She saw that quite clearly. She had been blind. She was engaged to Hugo when Will came home and she had been so besotted with Hugo that she had neglected Will completely—and even

211

after she had broken her engagement she had still been blind. She remembered the conversation on the night of Julie's arrival and how Julie had said, "He is like a brother still?" and she had replied that he was. "That is what I wanted to know," Julie had explained. It was obvious now why Julie had wanted this piece of information.

Patty looked back and tried to discover when this new feeling for Will had started, but somehow it didn't seem a "new feeling" at all. Perhaps she had really loved Will all the time. She had thought herself in love with Hugo, but she couldn't have been—not really—for it had all gone in a flash. Surely real love didn't vanish suddenly and completely and leave no regrets. ("Love suffereth long and is kind," thought Patty.) She bore no ill-will to Hugo, she didn't even blame him severely for the way he had treated her, for she realised it was not his fault. He was made like that. She had thought he was marvellous and had put him on a pedestal and when he had fallen off the pedestal—as idols sometimes do—she had discovered that she didn't love him.

Perhaps Patty might have suffered from regrets if it had not been for the stone. The day after Hugo had gone Patty found a curiously shaped stone in the car. She had lost a glove and when she was searching for it she had found a stone which had slipped down between the two front seats. It was a red stone with little flecks of mica which glittered in the sunshine like diamonds. She had seen it before of course; there was no mistaking it. For a few moments she held it in her hand and gazed at it incredulously and then she threw it away —and laughed. It didn't matter. It didn't make any difference to her feelings to discover that Hugo had told her a lie. *She just didn't care!*

Then Patty had thought, how strange! If I discovered that Will had told me a lie I would be horrified; I would be heart-broken . . . but of course Will wouldn't.

So perhaps she had really loved Will all the time!

Chapter 22

THERE HAD been a Girl Guide Meeting in the big hall at Torfoot Academy; it was over now, the girls had gone home rejoicing and their captain had been left to clear up the mess. The District Commissioner was there in an official capacity; also she had remained behind and was now offering her congratulations to the captain.

"Good show, Brenda," said Patty. "You've done a wonderful job with the company—smartened them up no end and put new life into them." She looked round the room and added, "But you should have made them stay and clear up."

Brenda flushed with pleasure to the roots of her mousy hair at this praise from her superior officer. "They're good material," she mumbled. "Just wanted a little ginger, that's all . . . and they offered to stay. I told them to make tracks because—well, because I wanted to talk to you, really. It won't take me long to stack the chairs and tidy up."

"I'll help——" began Patty, beginning to stack the chairs.

"You won't! Give me that chair, Patty! It isn't the thing for a District Commissioner——"

"Away!" laughed Patty.

"Put down that chair!"

" I won't! "

The two had behaved with admirable decorum for three solid hours. Brenda had presented her programme and marshalled her forces with aplomb; Patty had said a few well-chosen words and taken the company's salute. They were both suffering from reaction. Perhaps it was a little unfortunate that a child who had forgotten her gym-shoes and had returned to fetch them should have been a witness of the scene. The child stood at the door, mouth agape, amazed at the spectacle of the captain and the District Commissioner fighting like a couple of tigers over the possession of a tubular chair. Then she turned and fled so swiftly and silently that the combatants never saw her—but the news went all round the company like wild-fire!

" Patty, for goodness' sake! " cried Brenda, half laughing and half in earnest. " I can do it in five minutes —well, ten perhaps—and I'd much rather if you don't mind. Do please sit down and talk. I want to talk to you about something special."

Thus adjured the District Commissioner straightened her tie, smoothed her curls, which had become disarranged in the unseemly struggle, and sat down upon a coil of rope which had been used for an exhibition of rope-climbing.

" All right," she said. " If the little wretches have left any lemonade I'll have some. If not you can get me a glass of water out of the tap. All that talking has made me as dry as a lime-kiln."

There was no lemonade, of course; there never was a drop of lemonade nor a crumb of biscuit after the Torfoot Guides had slaked their appetites. Where they

put it their captain could not imagine. Brenda would
have fed her idol upon champagne and caviare if that
had been possible but as that was quite impossible at a
moment's notice she filled two glasses with water and
brought them in.

The District Commissioner accepted hers without
comment—she had not really expected lemonade. " Well,
what is it? " she asked. " Another bright idea from
headquarters? "

" Come to London with me," said Brenda. " No,
don't say you can't without thinking. I really mean it.
You could get away perfectly easily for a few days and
it would do you good. It's years since you had a holiday
—literally years—isn't it? "

" Yes, but——"

" Your sister-in-law could look after everything.
Please, Patty. Please come—just for a few days. There's
a dance and lots of parties and we're going to a play.
I'm staying with the Murrays and they'd love to have
you."

" Why ever should they? "

" Because I've told them about you. I've told them
you're a wonderful person—and so you are. You're the
most wonderful person in the whole world," declared
Brenda, gazing at her idol with large beautiful grey eyes
which had suddenly become very soft and misty.

Few people can resist homage if offered sincerely—
and Patty was in a somewhat unstable condition. Her
heart was sore. She had been feeling that everything
was horrible. She had been " carrying on," of course,
laughing and talking and eating and drinking as usual
(because of course one had to) but she had not been

sleeping as usual in spite of the tisane. So, instead of turning aside the absurd compliment with a jest, she said rather huskily, " Oh, Brenda, if you only knew——"

" Perhaps I do know," said Brenda. " I've got eyes— and you're important to me."

" Brenda! Do I look——" began Patty in dismay.

" Not to other people. In fact Mrs. Hepburn said to-night that you seemed in particularly good form and of course I agreed."

" Well, that's a mercy! "

" You'll come, won't you, Patty? " asked Brenda returning to the attack. " I want you to come frightfully, and you'd like it when you got there, and even if you didn't enjoy it terribly much it would get you out of the bit. There's nothing like going away for a few days— different surroundings, different people! It gives you a different feeling if you have a chance to look at things from a distance. Oh, I can't explain what I mean! " declared Brenda in despair.

" I think you've explained it rather well," said Patty. She took a drink of water and added, " I could see what they say."

" Oh do! " cried Brenda joyfully. " The Murrays are nice—*really*—and they'd love to have you; not only because I've told them about you but because you're a sort of relation. I'm going on Tuesday; we can go together. It would be gorgeous. Julie could look after everything while you're away, couldn't she? "

" I suppose she could," said Patty a little doubtfully.

" Of course she could. She's a capable young woman and they like her—your parents, I mean. It's a heaven-sent opportunity for you to have a few days' holiday."

" Well, perhaps——"

" You'll bust up if you don't get away."

Patty considered the matter; (she knew that she had almost reached the limit of her endurance. It would be no help to anybody if she were to " bust up ") and the project which at first sight had seemed utterly impracticable began to seem quite feasible. How good it would be to get away from Langford, to look at her troubles from a distance! She realised that when she got back she might find that Will and Julie were engaged—but even that prospect was better than sitting at Langford waiting for it to happen.

2

Patty did not expect to enjoy her holiday in London (she was running away from Langford, not running to London for a round of gaieties) but the Murrays were so friendly and so obviously delighted to have her that only a " grim growdy " could have failed to appreciate their kindness.

Before Patty had been in the house an hour they had agreed that they were cousins; otherwise why should they all feel so completely comfortable together? This was quite enough proof of relationship with the younger members of the family. Further proof was provided by Mr. Murray who produced a small locket containing a miniature of his grandmother.

" It's my great-grandmother! " exclaimed Patty. " We've got a painting of her in the dining-room at Langford. That *absolutely* proves it."

Mr. Murray smiled and said that although it did not

absolutely prove the relationship in point of law, it was enough proof for any reasonably minded person. He added that the locket had belonged to his father; had been one of his father's dearest possessions.

" My father was a bit wild in his younger days," explained Mr. Murray. " He quarrelled with his family and went over to Canada in a huff determined to make his fortune. That's why he dropped the ' Elliot ' from his name and ceased to communicate with them. But he always had a soft spot for his mother, so he kept the little locket and eventually gave it to me. I've got one or two old letters and some day I should like to show them to Colonel Elliot Murray."

" You must," declared Patty. " Daddy will be frightfully interested."

This was all very pleasant—and other things were pleasant too. It was pleasant to share a room with Brenda and to listen to her confidences as they dressed. Brenda was " almost engaged " to Duncan Murray—and Patty was glad; Duncan was charming and would make a delightful husband for Brenda. Of course this meant that Brenda would leave Torfoot and live in London and Patty would miss her very much—so would the Torfoot Guides—but Brenda would be happy; that was the main thing.

" Why ' almost engaged '? " Patty wanted to know.

" I think Duncan is just waiting to see how he gets on in the firm," explained Brenda. " It's silly, of course, because I wouldn't mind a bit not having much money to start with. I mean—not with Duncan. I mean I would be quite happy in the tiniest little flat—with Duncan."

" It will be all right," declared Patty who had made her own observations on the state of affairs.

" You really think so? "

" Sure of it," said Patty.

3

Patty had not expected to enjoy the round of gaieties but she was sociably inclined and she had not visited London for years. It was fun to go shopping in the morning with Mrs. Murray; to rush home to lunch; to be taken to a party and then to a play and to finish the evening with supper in a fashionable restaurant. Patty had little time to think about Langford or to wonder what they were doing in her absence . . . and she found she was so tired with all the rush and bustle that she fell into her comfortable bed and slept soundly.

The dance was a prodigious affair. It was being held in a large house in Park Lane which belonged to some relations of Mrs. Murray's. The Murrays had a dinner party beforehand so Patty did not lack partners. The young man who had taken her in at dinner—and whose name was Allen Something (Patty never knew what!) was an excellent dancer and his step fitted Patty's to perfection. They danced together most of the evening. Patty also danced with Duncan and was told in strictest confidence that he had just asked Brenda to marry him and she had said yes—and it was the most wonderful, joyful thing that had ever happened . . . so Patty congratulated him and told him that Brenda was a perfect darling. Duncan had known this before but was delighted to have his opinion confirmed.

"Yes, isn't she?" agreed Duncan enthusiastically. "And she's so beautiful—at least I think so."

Patty thought so too. "Beautiful eyes," she said.

"Absolutely beautiful."

They were in complete accord.

"I'm doing quite well in the firm," continued Duncan. "Father says so—and he wouldn't say it unless it was true—so we'll be able to have quite a nice little flat. When you come to London—any time—you must come and stay. We're cousins—and Brenda thinks the world of you," he added.

Patty was so enchanted with the news of Duncan and Brenda's engagement that when she met Cousin Hugo face-to-face coming out of the supper-room she was able to take him in her stride; she was able to smile at that marvellous young man's discomfiture. Of course Patty had a slight advantage over Hugo, for she was aware that he went about a good deal and it had crossed her mind that she might meet him in London. It was not likely of course—London is a very big place—but it was possible. In Hugo's case the encounter was entirely unexpected (he could not have been more astonished if he had met a lady from Mars) so, instead of passing by with an icy stare of unrecognition, he stood stock still and gaped like a cod-fish.

"Patty!" he exclaimed. "What on earth are you doing here!"

"Dancing," replied Patty cheerfully. "It's a lovely party, isn't it?" She added, "Oh, by the by, Hugo, I found something belonging to you at Langford after you had gone."

"Something belonging to me?"

" It was in the car. I didn't bother to send it to you—
I didn't think you would want it."

" You didn't think——"

" No," said Patty. " You see it was only a funny
little red stone with glitters in it. I'm afraid I threw it
away but I dare say I could find it if you want it as a
keep-sake."

Hugo was dumb. It was the only time Patty had
ever seen him dumb. Usually Hugo had plenty to say.

" It's my dance, Patty," said Allen Something's
voice in her ear and she was swept away before Hugo
had time to recover.

Afterwards when Patty thought about it she was surprised at herself—and a trifle ashamed. She was glad
she had told him, for it was just as well he should know,
but she could have told him more gently. There had
been no need to rub it in.

Chapter 23

THINGS SEEMED much the same at Langford when Patty returned after her visit to London. All had gone well under Julie's management. Tom greeted her with the proud news that he could now ride Scottie by himself and could go in and out of the obstacles in the paddock which had been placed there for the purpose. Her father seemed in good form and her mother less muddled than usual. Patty had a feeling that Julie was slightly under the weather but put it down to the weight of responsibilities which had rested upon her shoulders. Patty asked twice if there were any interesting news but apparently there was none—except a few items of gossip about the neighbours.

" Brenda Heston is engaged—but of course you know about that," said the Colonel. " Oh, and Arbuthnot rang up to say everything is O.K. and he's writing to Hugo."

" What are you talking about, Thomas? " asked Mrs. Elliot Murray waking suddenly from her dreams.

" Just business, my dear," replied the Colonel quickly.

" But why should Mr. Arbuthnot write to Hugo? "

" About a matter of business. It's nothing important. You wouldn't understand, my dear."

" Have you seen Will lately? " asked Patty. She had

not intended to say it but it had become second nature to say the first thing that came into her mind to guide her mother away from a danger zone—and Will was the first thing in her mind.

" Not for a day or two," the Colonel replied. " He's away just now—gone to shoot with those cousins of his in Perthshire."

" You've been away too, haven't you, Patty? " said Mrs. Elliot Murray vaguely. "Did you go to Perthshire with Will? "

" No, darling. You know I didn't. I was in London with Brenda. I told you——"

" Oh yes, I remember now, but I think it would have been much more enjoyable if you had gone with Will."

" We had a lovely time," declared Patty. " The Murrays couldn't have been kinder——"

" So of course they're your cousins," suggested the Colonel with a smile.

" They really are, Daddy. Mr. Murray is going to write to you and explain all about it. . . ."

All this was so much as usual that when bedtime came Patty felt as if she had never been away at all, and this feeling was intensified when she went along to Julie's room and found her sitting up in bed drinking tisane.

" I hope it wasn't too much for you," said Patty as she settled herself comfortably on the end of the bed and took up the second cup which was standing on the table steaming gently.

" It was not too much at all, but I missed you badly and I am glad you have come back to Langford." She

added, " Will you make reservations for me, Patty
dear? "

" Reservations? "

" Tickets and things," explained Julie. " I am going
home. It is difficult for me to telephone and if you will
do it for me it will be so very kind."

Patty hesitated. She was anxious to know Julie's
plans but she was almost afraid to ask. At last she said,
" But of course you'll be back soon."

" I am not coming back at all."

" Julie! What do you mean? "

" I am going home," repeated Julie. " It is best for
everyone that I should go—and not come back. Oh, it
is not a sudden thought. It is a thought that has been
growing in my head for nearly two weeks. You have
been very kind and nice to me and I love you all but it
is not sensible for me to stay. Tom will stay at Langford. You will be good to him I know, so I will not
ask you that."

Patty gazed at her in amazement. She was sitting up
in bed with the fleecy shawl round her shoulders; she
was holding the cup in her hands; her eyes were fixed
on the contents of the cup as though she were reading
her fortune; her face, usually so round and comely,
was pinched and drawn like the face of an old woman.

" Julie, what has happened! You can't mean it! "
cried Patty. "You wouldn't go away and leave Tom! "

" Please—do not talk of that," said Julie in a queer
strained voice. " I will try to explain a little and you
will say nothing—no nothing. If you are sorry for me
I shall cry—and that will be silly. I am trying so hard
to be sensible."

Patty said nothing.

" I have thought and thought," continued Julie. " It has not been easy. Whatever I do is sad . . . but I see now it is best for everyone if I go away. It is best for Tom. He will be sad when I go away but he will not be sad for long. His place is here. Tom must grow up at Langford. Will said that long ago and I did not understand, but now I can see it is true."

" Oh, Julie! "

" Please, Patty! I have told you not to be sorry. It is because we are friends that I am trying to explain. To the others we will say I am going to Nivennes to see my mother and make plans and they will think I am coming back so they will not mind at all. To you I will tell the truth—because we are friends—because I want you to help me and to make it easy." She gave a little sob and added, " You are good at making things easy, Patty dear. You make things easy for everyone all the time."

Patty had been told not to speak so she was silent and after a few moments Julie continued more calmly. " It is best for Tom that I should go away—he will settle down more quickly—and it is best for me too. I will go back to my own place and my own people. For a time I shall be sad but afterwards I shall be quite contented. There will be a great deal to do, and that is what I like."

" But Julie, there are things to do here, at Langford."

" There is not enough to do here—and to tell the truth I am not very happy at Langford. In a little while I think I might be very unhappy indeed and that would not be a good thing for anybody."

"Oh Julie, we've tried to make you happy."

"I know you have tried—and you have all been very kind. You could not have been kinder. It is not your fault at all . . . but there are all sorts of things that make me not very happy."

"What things?" asked Patty anxiously.

"I do not like your weather," Julie replied.

Patty almost smiled. It seemed an anti-climax—and as a matter of fact she was surprised, for the weather had been extremely kind to Julie and Tom. Ever since they came it had been mild and mellow, with morning mist in the hollows which had cleared away in the gentle warmth of the autumn sun.

"Perhaps it is rude and you are cross?" asked Julie in some concern.

"No, of course not," said Patty hastily. "Not cross at all—just surprised. Does the weather matter so much?"

"Perhaps it is a small thing," admitted Julie. "But life is made up of a lot of small things. I miss the hot golden sunshine and the bright colours of the flowers and I miss the people in the market—talking very fast and waving their hands and laughing—or perhaps getting a little cross when I drive a hard bargain. It is all so different here. It is not amusing to go marketing in Torfoot. The people here are nice and kind, but they are so quiet. All your friends are nice and kind. Your friends ask me to go to tea and they talk to me with pleasant voices but all the same I do not belong. I am outside the fence. I am a stranger."

"They don't know you yet. It takes time——"

"They will never know me—and I will never know

them—never—not if I live here all my life," declared Julie.

She put her empty cup on the table beside her bed and drawing up her knees clasped her arms round them. It was one of her charms that she seemed so soft and pliable—almost as if she had no bones, thought Patty.

"These are all small things," said Julie thoughtfully. "It is difficult to talk about the bigger things, but perhaps you will understand without talking. That will be best."

Patty did not understand at all. "Are you going back to live with your mother?" she asked.

"For a little time. Then I will arrange myself."

"Arrange yourself?"

"Yes, there is no need for you to worry. It will be orlright."

"I don't know what you mean."

"It is time to think of the future," explained Julie. "I am not young any more and if I leave it any longer it will be too late. One must be sensible about these matters."

"Julie!" cried Patty. "Julie, you don't mean you're going to—to marry somebody—in Nivennes?"

Julie did not reply.

"Julie, I must know," urged Patty. "Please tell me. Is there somebody in Nivennes—somebody you're in love with?"

"I am not in love with anybody, Patty dear—but, yes, there is a man who would like me to be his wife. For a long time he has wanted me to marry him. My mother wanted me to marry him years ago, but I would not—

because of Tom. It would not have been a good thing for Tom."

Patty gazed at her speechlessly.

"You are surprised?" asked Julie. "Why should you be surprised? Listen, Patty, and I will tell you about André. He is tall and big and serious—and no longer young. Poor André, it is time he had a wife to take care of his house and to give him a family!" She sighed and added, "He is good and kind and he has been very patient. He has waited a long time. One could not expect him to wait much longer without knowing whether I will marry him or not."

Patty had listened to the description of André's virtues with growing astonishment and dismay. "Julie!" she cried. "A man like that—much older than yourself——"

"But, yes, of course he is older. He is an important person in Nivennes; he is the owner of a fine vineyard. The vineyard belonged to André's father and before that to his grandfather—the wine of the Delormes family is famous all over the district. André's house is large, it stands upon the hill above Nivennes and you can see the town from the windows. The rooms are very pleasant, especially the kitchen. The kitchen has big windows and a red brick floor. I shall have two young girls to help me but I shall do the marketing myself—and the cooking. There will be a great many things to do—but that is what I like—and they will be things that I know how to do. They will be things that I can do well."

"But you don't love him! How could you possibly ——"

"Oh, you are so romantic!" complained Julie. "I could never make you understand—never. Our ideas are different. I am not romantic—like you are."

"I know that of course. I mean I know marriages are 'arranged' in France, but——"

"If they are well arranged they are very happy indeed."

"But not you, Julie. You could never marry a man you didn't love, could you? It seems—it seems quite horrible."

"It does not seem horrible to me. To me it seems sensible and right to marry a good kind man, to be his wife and the mother of his children. It is because you are romantic——"

"But you're romantic!" cried Patty. "You and Rae —what could have been more romantic!"

For a few moments Julie was silent and then she said in a different tone, "Rae and I—yes, we were romantic. We loved each other and it was beautiful and happy—but there will never be another Rae. Rae was a prince in a fairy story." She gave a deep sigh and added, "I was young in those days. Now I am not young any more and it is time to be sensible and to make myself a new life."

During this long and intimate conversation there was one person who had not been mentioned. Patty had thought of him all the time but it seemed impossible to say his name. She looked at Julie—and wondered. She had been so sure that Will and Julie loved each other— but perhaps she had been mistaken! (I don't understand her at all, thought Patty. She said our ideas were different—and it's true. If I lived to be a hundred I

230

should never learn to understand her—so it's no good trying.)

"It is late," said Julie. "You are tired after your long journey, Patty dear. You must go to bed and sleep like a little mouse—and to-morrow you will telephone for me and make my reservations. I should like to go soon. I should like to go before Will comes home if that will be possible."

Patty kissed her and said good night and went away. She was certain she would not "sleep like a little mouse" but strangely enough she did.

Chapter 24

JULIE'S DECISION to go home to Nivennes did not disturb the other members of the household. She had said she would come for three weeks and she had stayed a month . . . and she was leaving Tom at Langford so of course she would come back. They all took that for granted. Even Tom was not unduly upset at the thought of his mother's departure. It seemed odd to Patty; but of course Patty knew (and it always seems odd, when we know something which other people do not, how other people can be so blind).

Patty telephoned, as requested, and worked out the details of Julie's journey. It was not an easy job; trains and planes had to be fitted together like a jig-saw puzzle, and Patty was no traveller. But at last she managed to arrange everything to her own satisfaction—and Julie's.

The day fixed for Julie's departure was the day of the Lanark Races and Tom, who was now a horseman, had been looking forward to his first race-meeting with keen anticipation.

" But of course you must go to the horse-races," declared his mother. " You must all go. There is no need for anyone to see me off. We can say ' adieux ' at Langford; it will be much nicer."

" We'll say ' au revoir'," said Colonel Elliot Murray smiling. " You mustn't stay away too long."

" Maman will come home soon," declared Tom cheerfully. " I would go with her to Nivennes to take care of her but it wouldn't be worth while for such a little time and Scottie would miss me dreadfully." He paused and added in a doubtful voice, " But Mamam, if you would like me to come to the station——"

Julie repeated her assurances that she wanted nobody to come to the station—and that was that.

Perhaps it was just as well, thought Patty. It was always a grim sort of business to see off people at a station whether they were coming back or not. She would go herself of course and if there were tears at the parting— her own tears or Julie's—nobody would be any the wiser.

It was a perfect autumn morning when they left Langford to drive over to the little station on the main line. The trees were bare by this time, their leaves lay round about them making carpets of gorgeous colourings on the ground. The sky was pale blue with a few little fleecy clouds which moved slowly, trailing their shadows over the hills. Mist was rising from the river; dewdrops sparkled on the grass.

" It is pretty—yes," said Julie as she came down the front doorsteps muffled in scarves. " It is very pretty to look at, but there is no warmth in the sun. I cannot understand why the sun should shine without any warmth in it. Some day you will come and visit me at Nivennes and you will see what I mean."

Very little was said during the drive—nothing of importance—but at the station they had a little time to wait and as they walked up and down the platform Patty made up her mind to speak. It was impossible to let Julie go like this—without knowing.

" What am I to say to Will? " asked Patty.

" There is nothing to say," said Julie in a very small voice. " He will not be surprised when he comes back from his cousins and finds I am not here."

" No message at all? "

" No message—except you can say I am hoping he is a very good prophet and some day André will have a son who will grow up at Nivennes and learn how to make golden wine."

" Julie! What does it mean? "

" It is a joke," said Julie with a little sob. " Tell Will it is a joke. He will understand."

The train came in at that moment and Julie was suddenly weeping. She clung to Patty and whispered incoherently, " Oh Patty, you are so kind to me! You are like Rae—perhaps that is why I love you so much— I love you so very much—do not forget me altogether, Patty dear. Think well of me—or as well as you can. You do not understand me at all—but you love me a little bit, n'est-ce pas? "

" I love you a lot! " murmured Patty hugging her tightly.

" Be happy," sobbed Julie. " Be happy. That is all I want. I am silly to cry. It is the best thing—best for everybody—best for me too—so you must not feel unhappy—you must not worry. I shall be orlright."

The train only stopped for a few minutes and somehow or other Julie was bundled in before it steamed off to London. Patty watched till it was out of sight and then turned and groped her way back to the car through a blinding mist of tears.

2

Several days passed. Julie's absence left a large gap in the Langford household for she had done a great many little jobs in an unobtrusive way, and everybody had become very fond of her; but everybody, Tom included, made the best of it and talked quite happily of her return.

" It's Grandmaman," explained Tom. " She would like Maman to stay for ever and ever at Villa des Cygnes but of course Maman won't do that so we needn't worry."

" She'll have a lot of arrangements to make," said Colonel Elliot Murray. " I don't suppose she'll be able to come home before Christmas."

" Christmas is a long way off," said Tom rather wistfully. " But—yes—there will be a lot to do. Perhaps Maman will sell Villa des Cygnes and Grandmaman will go to Marseilles and live with Tante Louise—or perhaps Tante Louise will go to Villa des Cygnes."

Patty took no part in these conversations and the secret, which lay heavy on her shoulders, remained a secret. How long it would remain a secret she could not tell. Julie might wait until she had "arranged herself" and then write and break the news, or she might allow things to drift in the hope that the Elliot Murrays would realise the truth for themselves . . . but what about Will? Did Will know or not, wondered Patty.

On Saturday when Patty went home after a morning's shopping in Torfoot she saw Will's car in the drive. She was a little late so they had started lunch without her and when she went into the dining-room they were all sitting round the table. Will greeted her in his usual friendly manner and replied to her questions by saying he had had several good days on the moors and had shot none too badly.

"Will brought us two brace of grouse," said the Colonel smiling.

"And a pheasant," said Tom. He laughed and added, "Pheasants don't live on the hills. I thought they did —but I've learnt a lot since I came home to Langford."

It was true that Tom had learnt a lot, he was soaking up knowledge like a sponge. They had decided to keep him at Langford until he had learnt more about the manners and customs of his father's country and then send him to school. Meanwhile a suitable tutor must be found: a young graduate if possible, a man who would take an interest in the unusual job of teaching a boy who had been brought up in France and gone to a French school. Miss Vernon had taught him to speak English but she had not bothered much about writing and grammar so there were large gaps in Tom's knowledge which must be filled.

Patty thought of all this as she took her usual place at the table beside her mother and began to eat her lunch. She glanced at Will several times and saw that he looked quite cheerful so she decided that he did not know about Julie. He must know she had gone, of course, but like the others he expected her to come back. Later, if she could get Will alone, she would have to give him Julie's parting message. Patty did not want to give it to him. The message meant little to her but she supposed Will would understand it and be enlightened.

Chapter 25

WHEN PATTY had finished clearing the luncheon-table (a duty which Julie had undertaken but which now reverted to Patty) she went to look for Will. The message must be delivered, and the sooner the better. She searched the house and the garden, but she could not find him, and if his car had not been standing in the drive she would have given it up in despair. Then suddenly she remembered the play-room—and there she found him sitting at the table cleaning the little gun. He looked up as she went in and she saw that there was a smear of oil across his forehead and another on the collar of his shirt.

"Oh, you're cleaning the little gun!" said Patty. It was a silly thing to say (quite futile, really, and she had an odd sort of feeling that she had said it before) but she had to say something; she could not blurt out Julie's message without any preliminaries at all.

"I thought I'd better," Will replied. "Tom wants to shoot so I thought I'd take him out on Monday and give him a lesson."

Patty went to the window and looked out. "Julie has gone," she said.

"I know," said Will.

"She left a message for you. It's a cryptic sort of

message but she said you would understand. I was to tell you that she hoped you were a good prophet and that some day there would be a son for André Delormes —a son who would grow up at Nivennes and learn how to make golden wine."

" Gosh! " exclaimed Will in amazement. " Gosh, what on earth——"

" She said you would understand," repeated Patty. " She said it was a joke. Don't you know what it means? "

" Let me think," said Will vaguely. " Yes, I believe I did say something like that. When was it? Oh yes, it was after that frightful meal when Madame Leyrisse was so rude. Julie and I were standing at the gate and I was trying to make her see why it was so important for Tom to grow up at Langford. I told her to put things back to front. I asked her if André Delormes would like his son to grow up in England, not knowing anything about his business, or whether it would be better for him to grow up in Nivennes and learn how to make golden wine. Julie saw the idea."

Patty saw the idea too (she knew all about Will's curious method of solving difficult problems); she also saw exactly what Julie had meant by her message to Will. The strange thing was Will did not seem to mind.

" Aren't you—upset about it? " she asked, turning from the window and gazing at him in surprise.

" I was a bit upset," he admitted. " I was angry and—and baffled. I couldn't understand her at all. That's why I went north to stay with the Jardines. I just felt I had to get away. Shooting isn't as good as fishing for thinking things out but it's a help to get right away from things."

" To look at things from a distance," murmured Patty.

He nodded. " Yes, you can get things in perspective. I began to see that it was all for the best."

" All for the best! You mean Julie going away and——"

" Yes, it's the best for everybody really. Tom will feel it at first but he'll soon settle down—he's settling down already—and Julie will be happier at Nivennes. Julie loves the hot golden sunshine. I remember one day when the sun was absolutely baking and I was thankful to sit in the shade I saw her walking about in the sun with no hat. She's a Child of the Sun."

" I feel awfully miserable about her," said Patty.

Will put down the gun and leaned his elbows on the table. " I don't think you need," he said thoughtfully. " People must choose for themselves; they must make their own lives. Julie has chosen to be amongst her own people. I've thought about her a lot, you know. Sometimes I've thought she still loves Rae so much that she will never really love anybody else. Sometimes I've thought that she's selfish——"

" Oh no! "

" Well, perhaps not selfish exactly. I mean she thinks of herself and of her own future."

" We all do, more or less."

" Oh, I don't blame her," declared Will. " It's sensible to think of the future. Julie realised she couldn't settle down here and be happy so she decided to cut her losses and go back to France."

"Yes," agreed Patty doubtfully. "But that's not all. I believe there's something else—something we haven't thought of—I'm terribly fond of Julie, but I don't understand her one little bit."

"That's part of the trouble—none of us understands her, and I don't believe we ever could. I've tried putting her back to front; for instance would you like to spend the rest of your life at Nivennes amongst people who didn't understand you?"

"No!" exclaimed Patty.

"Well, you see what I mean."

Patty saw. She thought, but I couldn't marry a man unless I loved him, no matter how good and kind he was.

"Listen, Patty," said Will. "I want you to know the whole thing. I thought I was in love with Julie—and I was almost certain that she felt the same about me. In fact I thought it was—practically—settled. So it was a bit of a shock when I asked her to marry me and she said no."

Patty had turned and was gazing out of the window . . . So I was right, she thought, or at least partly right. He really was in love with Julie!

"Julie said a most extraordinary thing," added Will in a surprised sort of voice. "She said, ' love is very nice but life goes on for a long time.' "

He paused for a moment but Patty made no comment.

"I was baffled," declared Will. "I told her I didn't understand what she meant, but she didn't explain. She just said she wasn't very happy here and in a little while she might be very unhappy indeed and that wouldn't be a good thing for anybody, so she was going home to Nivennes 'to arrange herself.' "

(She had said the same to Patty in almost exactly the same words. It was a queer experience to hear Julie's words falling from Will's lips like this.)

" Then," continued Will. " Then, when I pressed her further about her plans, I found they were all cut and dried. She had decided to marry André Delormes . . . and she proceeded to tell me how important he was in Nivennes, and what a nice house he had——"

" The kitchen has big windows and a red brick floor," murmured Patty.

" Yes, she said that," agreed Will. " She said that—and a whole lot more. It was all so sensible and matter-of-fact that it sort of—sort of disgusted me. I never thought Julie was—was like that. It was an eye-opener to me."

He took up the little gun and went on with his task.

" She isn't really ' like that '," said Patty thoughtfully. " I mean she isn't hard-boiled. She cried dreadfully when she went away. It's just that she wants that kind of life and she knows she could do it well. It's sensible and——"

" It's far too sensible," declared Will. " It takes all the glamour out of life to be too sensible. It makes life awfully hum-drum. I thought Julie was glamorous; she looks soft and beautiful like a ripe apricot, but there's a hard stone inside. I suppose you'll say I ought to have expected to find a stone inside an apricot. "

Patty had no intention of saying any such thing. Her fingers had begun to fiddle with the cord of the blind and it seemed that this was absorbing all her attention.

"Well, there it is," said Will. "That's what happened. At the time I was upset and angry—as I told you—and then I found I was glad. It was a relief. I found I didn't want to marry Julie; I found I wasn't in love with her at all. It sounds quite mad, I know, but it's the absolute truth. She's going to marry André Delormes, not because she loves him—I could have understood that—but because he can give her the sort of life she wants. It may be sensible but it puts me off completely."

"I hope she'll be happy," said Patty softly.

"So do I—but it seems quite horrible to me."

"It isn't horrible to her. Julie has been brought up to think it's the right thing to do, so it seems quite natural to her."

"Yes, it's just that our ideas are different. She's not romantic—like we are."

(That was exactly what Julie had said to Patty: "Our ideas are different. I am not romantic—like you are.")

"I suppose we are—romantic," said Patty doubtfully.

"I don't know whether we are or not. I *do* know that I'm a perfect fool," declared Will emphatically.

Patty's fingers were very busy tying knots in the blind cord, but although she did not look up from her ridiculous employment she was aware that Will had risen from the table and had come over to the window.

"Patty, I'm a perfect fool," he repeated. "It's you I love. It's you I want to marry."

She could not speak. She was tying knots as though her life depended upon it.

Suddenly Will's hands closed over hers tightly. "It's

242

you," he said. " It's been you all the time—and I didn't know! Could you possibly marry a perfect fool? "

" Oh Will! " she whispered. " I've been a fool too. I thought I loved Hugo. Oh Will, how could I have been such an idiot."

She turned and buried her face against his shoulder and his arms went round her. The blind came down with a clatter and lay in ruins at their feet.

" Oh dear! " cried Patty laughing hysterically. " Oh goodness, what a fright it gave me! Rae always said——"

Envoi

Monsieur Benoit was standing upon the steps of his hotel in the afternoon sunshine watching the world go by. Business was slack—it was out of season—as a matter of fact the hotel business was never very brisk in Nivennes. Tourists flocked to better-known towns; towns where there were ancient churches or some other inducement for sightseers. There was nothing in Nivennes except the market. Monsieur Bénoit was fond of Nivennes but he was wondering whether it would be a good plan to sell the hotel for what he could get—which would not be much—and accept the offer of his brother. His brother was the owner of a small hotel at Cannes and was lining his pockets rapidly. His brother had suggested that Monsieur Bénoit should join him as a junior partner. Would it be better to be a junior partner in a going concern or remain monarch of all he surveyed in a concern which was slowly but surely declining?

He was considering the matter seriously—and rather sadly—when he saw an automobile approaching. It was a moderately sized vehicle but it was new and shiny and bore the letters G.B.; there were a lady and a gentleman in the front seat and the tonneau was full of luggage —so Monsieur Bénoit was delighted when the vehicle slowed down and stopped before the entrance of the hotel. His expression changed in a moment and his podgy face was all smiles as he ran down the steps to greet his visitors.

" Bonjour, Monsieur Bénoit," said the gentleman removing his dark glasses and holding out his hand. " You have not forgotten me, I hope."

" Monsieur 'Astee! " cried Monsieur Bénoit. " No indeed I have not forgotten you! What pleasure to see you again! You are staying with us? "

" You have a room? "

" But yes—of course! A delightful room! It is next-door to the room you had before. So quiet and so convenient—"

" This is Madame Hastie."

Monsieur Bénoit smiled and bowed and declared himself enchanted.

" You would like some tea," said Monsieur Bénoit, who had suddenly remembered the curious taste of his guest. " It will be ready in a few moments; I will attend to it myself."

" You see? " said Will Hastie, smiling at his wife.

She laughed. " Well, it *will* be rather nice," she declared. " I must say I *crave* for a cup of tea at this hour in the afternoon."

Will and Patty had made plans several times to visit Nivennes but each time their plans had fallen through for some reason or another. Now they were old married folk; they had been married for two years and possessed a daughter but as she was still too young to enjoy a trip to France they had left her behind. There had been some talk of bringing Tom to visit his mother but

STILL GLIDES THE STREAM

eventually it had been decided not to. Patty was making a reconnaissance—she would see how the land lay—and if it seemed desirable Tom could visit his mother later. The fact was she had lost touch with Julie; she had written to Julie quite often but had received very few letters in reply—and it is difficult to carry on a one-sided correspondence.

Will and Patty were too tired to do anything on the evening of their arrival except to unpack and go to bed, but the next morning—after a breakfast of bacon and eggs—they felt a great deal better. Patty had expected Will to come with her to visit the Delormes but at the last minute Will cried off.

"You go," said Will. "You'll get more out of her if I'm not there. To tell you the truth I'm not very keen to see her."

Patty was extremely anxious to see Julie, she felt quite excited at the idea, but she realised that it was different for Will so she did not try to persuade him.

2

There was no difficulty in finding the Delormes's place. The house stood on the side of the hill and could be seen for miles; all round it were terraces with vines growing on them in orderly rows. Quite a lot of people were working amongst the vines, mostly women and girls in brightly coloured overalls and head-scarves. They waved to Patty as she passed and Patty returned the greeting. It was all very pretty, and very "foreign" to Patty's eyes.

The road led to a big yard paved with stones. Patty

switched off the engine but did not get out of the car
at once. She sat and looked round her. The yard was
surrounded with white-washed buildings, so white that
they dazzled the eyes; the paint upon doors and windows and shutters was new and shiny; everything was
clean and neat—it all looked prosperous. Now that she
was actually here she had a sudden qualm of appre-
hension . . . perhaps she should have warned Julie of
her visit! She had thought it would be fun to take Julie
by surprise—but now she was not sure—it was so long
since she had heard from Julie. But it was too late
now so she must just go through with it. She wondered
whether she should call at the front door in formal
style, but that seemed silly! The back door opened on
to the yard; it stood ajar and she heard the sound of
people moving about inside—the sound of voices and
the clank of dishes.

Pull up your socks and don't be an idiot, said Patty
to herself, and with that she jumped out of the car and
knocked. The door was flung wide open—and there
was Julie.

"Patty!" cried Julie in amazement. "Oh Patty, is
it really you! Oh, Patty, how lovely!"

There was no doubt about her welcome. They were
in each other's arms in a moment, locked in an affec-
tionate embrace.

"Oh, what a delightful surprise! Dear Patty, how
good it is to see you! I have thought of you so much!
Oh, I know I have been very wicked not to write, but
the days go by and I am so busy—and I am not good
at writing letters. When I have found a pen and the
ink and composed myself to write there is something

else to be done which must be done at once . . . or
someone comes and I must speak to them . . . or there
is a message for André on the telephone . . ."

" I know," agreed Patty laughing. " But surely a
postcard——"

" No, no! " cried Julie, opening her eyes very wide.
" A postcard would not have been a good thing, for the
postman would have seen the wrong spelling! But
come in, dear Patty! You will not mind coming into
the kitchen? I cannot trust Suzette to cook the dinner
properly without supervision and André is bringing
home a guest."

Patty did not mind at all. She followed her hostess
into the kitchen. She was interested, though not surprised, to see that the kitchen was large and bright, with
big windows and a red brick floor. The windows were
open and had red and white checked curtains which
moved gently in the breeze. There were two wooden
tables, their tops scrubbed white and smooth as satin,
and a large stove with pots simmering on the top; there
was a huge old-fashioned dresser with blue and white
china, and several long shelves, stacked with gleaming
pots and pans.

Beneath the window was a row of sinks and here
stood a girl peeling potatoes. Patty saw that she was
quite a young girl but already she was running to fat—
with a back like a cart-horse! As she stooped over the
sink her cotton dress cocked up behind and displayed
two extremely solid legs. " Let us sit down," said
Julie, drawing up a wooden chair and arranging a cushion
in it. " There is so much to say—so much that I want
to ask you. Suzette will not bother us for she is very

248

stupid and she has not one word of English so it will be just like being alone."

Hearing her name, Suzette looked round and smiled. Her smile was a little spoilt by the fact that one of her front teeth was missing, leaving an unsightly gap.

"Bonjour, Suzette," said Patty in her usual friendly way.

Suzette did not reply.

" She is very stupid—as I told you," explained Julie. " But she does what I tell her and she is not cheeky. I have another girl as well—she is more intelligent but does not always do as she is told."

" You can't have everything," said Patty laughing.

" Oh, Patty, it is so lovely to see you and to hear your laugh. It reminds me of happy times at Langford. It reminds me of the evenings when you sat on my bed and we drank tisane. You will stay to lunch, I hope; I want you to meet André."

Patty explained that this was just a flying visit but she would come back some other time. It was difficult to refuse the invitation without giving offence, for as a matter of fact she had no reasonable excuse, but eventually after some argument she agreed to stay and meet André and drink a glass of wine before taking her departure.

" That will be better than nothing," declared Julie with a sigh.

" How's your mother? " asked Patty. " Does she still live at Villa des Cygnes? "

" No, indeed! " cried Julie. " She has left Nivennes more than a year ago and has gone to stay at Marseilles with her sister. They do not get on very well, in fact they quarrel all the time, but they both enjoy quarrelling so it does not matter. It is something for them to do," added Julie quite seriously. " Life would be very boring for them without their little quarrels."

Patty hid a smile. She had heard quite a lot about Madame Leyrisse from Will and could imagine the cat and dog existence led by the two sisters. She said, " And what about Miss Vernon? I'm hoping to see her——"

" I am afraid that is impossible. Poor Miss Vernon has been very, very ill, but she is getting better now. Soon she will be well enough to come here and stay with us. André has agreed—he is so kind—and it will be lovely for me to be able to take care of her and so repay a little her goodness. Oh, she enjoys her radio-gram, it has been a great blessing during her illness, but that was really from Will and not from me."

They went on talking but in spite of all the interesting things they had to say Julie did not forget her duties. She rose several times to stir a pot or adjust the heat of the oven and once she rushed into the back-kitchen with a swirl of her skirt to demand why Marie was idling when there was so much to be done. Did not Marie know the time? asked her mistress. Was she not aware it was already eleven o'clock and the floor unwashed? And what of the stairs? Would the stairs clean themselves while Marie gossiped at the door with Alphonse?

During this interlude Suzette looked round—and winked—and remarked in her own language, " She has eyes in the back of her head—that one."

Patty did not reply—it was difficult to know what to say—but the thought crossed her mind that perhaps Suzette was not as stupid as Julie imagined.

In a few moments Julie returned from her sally. "Tell me about Tom," she said. "I have been talking all the time, it is your turn now."

"Tom is very well," Patty replied. "He has grown a lot——"

"His grandfather is pleased with him?"

"Oh yes, he thinks there's nobody in the world like Tom."

"He spoils Tom a little?" asked Tom's mother anxiously.

"Perhaps—a little," agreed Patty. "But it doesn't matter. You see Tom is at school now, so he gets well disciplined. It's a delightful school called Summerhills which belongs to Will's friend, Roger Ayrton—and it's very convenient. I mean it's not far from Langford so Tom comes home quite often for a week-end. There are about thirty boys in the school and Tom has lots of friends of his own age."

"He has learnt to play cricket?"

"Yes," said Patty smiling at the question. "At least he's learning to play cricket and football, and he runs races at the sports."

"Just like an English boy," said his mother nodding. She sighed and added, "It was right for me to leave him and come away."

"You never regretted it?"

"Oh yes," declared Julie frankly. "I was very sad to leave him—as you know—but it was all in the pattern. If I had stayed at Langford it would have twisted the pattern out of shape. I did not fit in."

So far they had not mentioned Mrs. Elliot Murray. Julie knew already that she had died, for Patty had written and told her, but now Julie wanted to know more.

" I was a little sad when I got the letter," said Julie. " She was so kind to me and so gentle. Nobody could be very sad, could they, Patty dear? "

This was true, of course. Nobody could feel very sad about her passing but she had left an unexpectedly big gap in the lives of her family and her friends. The mists in which she had dwelt for so long had thickened round her and she had drifted away quite peacefully.

" Rae was there," said Patty. " Just at the end Mummy saw him and held out her arms. He really was there, Julie."

" Dear Patty, I am sure he was! "

They were silent for a few moments and then Julie continued, " I think very often of Rae. Although he left me so long ago he is still part of the pattern of my life."

" You mean you would have been—different—if it had not been for Rae."

" That—yes—and more," said Julie in a very low voice. " Often I remember things that Rae said to me. He was so wise. It was because of Rae that I left Langford and came home to Nivennes."

" Because of Rae? " asked Patty in surprise.

Julie nodded. " Oh, there were other things as well: the sun was not warm and the people were strange and I had not enough to do, but these things were small and in time I might have got used to them. The big reason why I made up my mind to leave Langford and come home was because of Rae. It was because of something he said to me long ago. I can tell you about it now—for it will not matter—I could not tell you at the time." She hesitated for a moment and then added, "Rae was talking about you and Will, he said that some day you would discover you were in love with each other."

"Julie!"

Julie nodded gravely. "Yes, he said that . . . and he was pleased. He said, ' Those two are made for each other—just like you and me—but they do not know it yet.' At first, when I saw you and Will, I thought it was not true. I thought Rae was wrong. You and Will were good friends—just like brother and sister—but afterwards I changed my mind and I saw Rae was right. It was not as a brother and sister that you loved each other. That was the big reason why I came away."

"Oh, Julie!" cried Patty in dismay.

"There is no reason to be sad—none at all," declared Julie. "We are all quite happy and comfortable. You and Will are happy—and so is Tom. André is happy too. André is well-contented with his wife. He is so good to me—dear André—and he thinks all I do is right. He thinks all the changes I have made in his house are changes for the better . . . and it is true," added Julie frankly. "His house was not at all well cared for until I came."

Patty could not speak. She did not know whether she wanted to laugh or cry.

"So it is orlright," continued Julie. "It is orlright for everybody. Soon there will be another change in André's house—and that, too, will be for the better. Soon there will be a son for André. Will was a very good prophet, you see."

" Oh, Julie, I'm so glad."

" Yes, it is nice."

" A son—or perhaps a daughter," suggested Patty.

" It will be a son—for André," Julie declared. " That is in the pattern. Later there will be a daughter—for me."

Patty believed her. Indeed it was impossible not to believe her. She was so sure of herself—so sure that her life conformed with the pattern and the pattern was good. It was obvious that Julie was a round peg in a round hole. She was peaceful and contented. She was putting on weight. Quite soon (thought Patty) she would be too fat . . . but what did that matter? André would not mind.